HYDE COVE

JOSEPH PESAVENTO

COPYRIGHT

Cover design by Don Noble at Rooster Republic Press.

CONTENTS

To my hometown Marlboro, NY. You were a surplus of wonder and sadness. I'm glad I survived.

CHAPTER 1

RUNNING IN THE STORM

It was no later than nine in the evening during one of the decade's worst snowstorms. All the townspeople had gathered their groceries and hunkered down in their homes. The snow, after all, was some of the most eventful action they got in the tiny town of Hyde Cove. Snowplows were the only presence on the road as Jay Kirk strolled down the street to stop at a corner store. Wandering eyes peered out their windows, and Jay was unsure if they were in awe of the storm or in disgust of their town's pariah. A pack of smokes later, he made his way into the center of town with his crowbar ready. He stood outside of the bank, contemplating his next move. A move that would surely send him to County if he got caught doing something stupid again. Still, he knew he would have extra time if the roads were bad enough for the sheriff to leave early and head home. The storm was getting worse by the minute, and he'd been the only brave soul taking a chance outside.

Jay walked toward the entrance, slowly swinging the crowbar in his hand. He placed the tool between the two doors and pried, cracking the lock instantly. He didn't expect such ease with this move. Pushing the door open, he looked inside. He locked on to the blinking alarm and quickly played out his game plan in his head—rush the counter, empty any available cash, crack a few drawers, and then leave. Any mess-ups would void the extra time the snow bought him.

Jay took a breath and swung at the glass. The screeching alarm hardly slowed him as he reached in to unlock the door. He rushed to the counter and jumped over, immediately popping drawers open to grab anything available. He threw all the cash in a small drawstring bag draped around his shoulders and made his way to the exit. Jay glanced back to observe the fruition of the heist that he'd so carefully planned for several months. In fact, it was the last time he would see Hyde Cove. This money was for his new life.

Early in the previous year, Jay's dad Jerrod was caught with not only the largest possession of cocaine the state had ever seen but a handful of illegal firearms. Already widely known as the local fuck-up, Jerrod's domestic disputes and occasional barroom brawls had earned him countless police responses. Jerrod had similar aspirations of starting new, but his record stopped him from reaching better jobs due to his poor history. He became the sole provider of four children after their mother abandoned them. It was hard enough tolerating a man who couldn't get his life together, but it was especially difficult with four small mouths to feed.

Jay exited the bank and gave it an ironic salute followed by a middle finger high in the air. He estimated ten thousand dollars in his possession and was happy enough with that sum. A train ticket and a decent hotel room were all he looked forward to in the coming twenty-four hours. He'd toss a few thousand to the aunt he left his little brothers with. Jay told her he was taking the train down to the city for a few job interviews, but he was leaving them behind. His aunt was the only remaining family member with a decent name in their town. No one bothered her or spoke poorly of her, even if they didn't speak highly of her either. It was enough for Jay to leave them with some sort of adult for a proper upbringing.

Jay crossed the street and walked slowly down the sidewalk, admiring the quiet, snowy night. Another ten minutes went by without a single car on the road. The next vehicle to appear was a patrol car. He was confident he could talk his way out of getting into any trouble. He would tell them he was strolling home from a friend's place after a few drinks or that he went to get a quickie from a local girl the officer may or may not know. He wasn't worried.

The lights flashed on, and the car slowed as it approached. Jay realized he was still holding the crowbar and froze.

Sheriff Sullivan stepped out of the car. "To think I'd have an adventurous evening after going back to the precinct for forgetting something. Busy night, Jay?"

"No, Sheriff. Just had a few drinks at a friend's house. Walking it off," Jay said. He secreted the crowbar behind his right leg, thinking he was sly enough to pull it off.

Sheriff Sullivan closed his patrol car door and walked around the back. He stood a few feet from Jay. He eyed him up and down quickly and then smiled.

"The last thing I want to do right now is bring you in during this goddamn storm," Sheriff Sullivan said. "Why don't you tell me the truth, and we can go on with our night."

Jay knew it was over. Being honest would stall his plans, and a bold move on his part might get him clear of the Sheriff long enough to get on with his travels sooner. He weighed his options briefly and took a step toward the patrol car.

"I know it may look weird with the crowbar. My aunt locked a filing cabinet a few years ago and couldn't find the key. I was at a friend's house, really, and he lent me the crowbar to crack open the cabinet. What, do you think I robbed a bank or something?" Jay asked with a smile on his face.

"I don't even think you're dumb enough to do that with your kind of record," Sheriff Sullivan chuckled. "Go straight home. No need for any adventures in this weather."

"Absolutely. Have a good night, Sheriff," Jay said. He walked on, exhaling deeply with the assurance that his night, and now free life, had just gotten much better. He placed the crowbar on his shoulder and walked slightly faster than before.

Jay was in the clear. One more pit stop at home to grab his other bag, and he would make his way to the train station and head to the city. From there, he would find a destination suitable and affordable for his new life. As appealing as a city was to him, a vast and steady place for him to get lost in, a few thousand dollars wouldn't cover much of his expenses. He pondered the possibilities until he saw the flashing lights again. The same patrol car pulled up to him.

Sheriff Sullivan rolled down the window. "I got a call about the bank alarm going off. Does that seem familiar to you?"

Jay was once again stuck between two positions. He could talk his way out of it, but they'd eventually find a print proving he carelessly broke the door open without bothering to use gloves. He'd be stuck in jail until a judge gave him the long-awaited sentence he dreaded—the penitentiary. Jay had no backup plan, so he went the foolish route.

Neither Jay nor Sheriff Sullivan expected the crowbar to swing so fast. It was almost reactionary for Jay to slam the crowbar into the passenger's side of the cop car. Glass shattered all over Sheriff Sullivan's lap. Before he realized he would have to haul Jay in, his suspect was halfway down the block.

Goddamnit. Have it your way, Jay," Sheriff Sullivan said, pushing the gear into drive and turning on his siren. He reached for his radio while speeding down the road. "I need backup. In pursuit of a robbery suspect. Suspect's name is Jay Kirk. He could be armed."

Jay tried to take back alleys and stick to side streets. He weaved between parked cars and ran toward his apartment, where his other bag waited. All he needed to do was grab it, which coincidentally had one of his father's stolen firearms in it for safety, and he could be on his way to the train. Evading the sheriff and assuming backup was on their way was a distraction. He caught his breath at the end of the street and casually walked between houses for cover. Jay was roughly a block from his apartment when he saw a cop car parked outside with its lights flashing. He froze and then ducked between nearby houses.

"Fuck. How did they get here so fast?" he said. "Shit. Fuck it."

Jay walked on, staying low and avoiding any cars driving by. All he had to do was cross the Mill House Bridge, and he was home free. It was the line of jurisdiction for the local police, and it was just off the highway. Hitchhiking was readily available within ten or so feet. Jay's backup plan was to get to the bridge, lay low, and find an opportune window to flee and never look back. Before anyone had time to look for him, he would already be miles away, hitching a ride in the back of some station wagon.

There was about a mile between Jay's current location and the bridge. He hopped fences, ducked under parked cars, and crept around any sign of approaching vehicles. He was getting closer with few run-ins, so he stopped to take a breath. Then he saw the lights in his periphery again.

"Give it up, Jay. We have every cop available looking for you," Sheriff Sullivan said, leaning around the car beside Jay's cover, pistol drawn. "You can be better than *him*."

Jay knew right away that Sheriff Sullivan was referring to his father. He was aware that this would lead him down the same path, confirming the Kirk name was either cursed or spawned from rotten seed. Jay was ready to leave his name and reputation behind. Unlike his father, he wanted something better, despite the means he took to get there. Getting away from Hyde Cove was the start of leaving his father and his doings behind.

"I am better than him, Sheriff," Jay said. "Just let me be better than him." He crept away slowly, putting distance between them.

"You made your choice. You chose to take the dumb route. Make this easy for us, and we'll make it easier for you."

Jay was about ready to give up. He could see the edge of the river and the small street he needed to run down to get over the bridge. He was close enough to feel the excitement coursing through him. His head dropped, disappointed he got so close but not close enough to make it toward his new life. A rock rested between his feet. Just like the crowbar, Jay instinctively reached for it and tossed it at Sheriff Sullivan.

Jay heard the crack when the rock slammed into the sheriff's nose.

The sheriff dropped his gun and put his hands over his broken face to control the bleeding.

With the sheriff distracted by his injury, Jay had a moment of clarity. He rushed at Sheriff Sullivan and grabbed the gun from the ground. Then he ran as fast as possible toward the street leading to his freedom.

"Stop, Jay. I'll shoot if you don't stop," Sheriff Sullivan hollered. He wiped his nose on his sleeve and swung the car door open. Wadding several tissues to soak up the blood flowing freely from his nostrils, he drove in Jay's direction. "Can anyone get to Mill House Bridge? If we don't catch this asshole, he's history. Threw a rock at my face, and I'm gushing blood."

"On my way now, sir. I'll catch him," Officer Noah said. "On Western heading to Orange."

Officer Noah, one of the few black men in Hyde Cove, not even on the force for an entire year, had seen more action than some veterans. He'd arrested some of Jerrod Kirk's associates and taken a few down by force after one of them tried pulling a knife on him. Noah was polite and gentle but built like a linebacker, and he could handle himself in aggressive situations. After a mugger murdered his father, he devoted his life to stopping those who tried to hurt others while maintaining the integrity he believed an officer should always have. He took no interest or enjoyment in hurting people unless he felt his life was in grave danger.

Officer Noah pulled over when he saw Jay running toward the bridge. He immediately drew his pistol and headed after Jay.

"Stop, or I'll be forced to fire!" Officer Noah shouted.

Jay glanced at the officer while running and fired two rounds in his direction. The windshield caught the first round, and the second penetrated the car's hood. Officer Noah flinched and ducked. Jay continued to run, and Noah ran after him. Jay turned and fired again but didn't bother to aim. Noah ducked and continued his pursuit. Jay saw the bridge ahead, only twenty feet from his position.

"Jay, stop running, or I will use force!" Officer Noah yelled again.

He gained on Jay quickly. He was almost close enough to tackle him to the ground.

Jay reached back and fired again, clipping Officer Noah in the arm. The sound of the bullet ripping through flesh caused Jay to stop and look back.

Officer Noah gripped his weakened limb. His bicep poured blood down his sleeve. "Drop the gun, Jay. It's over."

"You can forget about me once I leave. I'm sorry. This is for the best," Jay said as he turned to finish his short run.

"Stop! Stop, Jay!" Officer Noah shouted as he aimed his gun.

Jay rushed at the final ten feet. Then he heard the shots echo from Noah's gun.

Bam!

The bullet pierced Jay's shoulder. He groaned, gripping below the bullet wound, but pushed on toward the bridge. Six feet away.

Bam!

The second shot grazed Jay's side. Blood leaked from his torn shirt. Three feet away.

Bam!

Jay turned to glance at Noah in his periphery. The bullet had torn through Jay's cheek and thrown him off balance. Blood sprayed from his face and painted the snow red beneath his feet.

Jay swayed and lost his balance while approaching the railing. He stumbled, leaning precariously over the side. Though he held on for several seconds, he fell to the dark, icy river below. Noah waited to hear a splash, but the sound never came. He stood and walked to the edge where the bridge met the guard rail.

Noah looked down to see the river running steadily. Large pieces of ice broke off from the bank and gradually drifted toward the edge of town. He noticed the blood from Jay's wounds, as it stood out in the large piles of white along the river's bank. If the fall hadn't killed Jay, the blood loss likely had. A crimson puddle stood out in Noah's view. He returned his pistol to the holster while Sheriff Sullivan approached in his car.

Tissues were shoved up the sheriff's nose to stop the bleeding. One of them was nearly soaked through to the bottom. Sheriff Sullivan walked to the guard rail where Noah stood looking down.

"Did he get away?" Sheriff Sullivan asked.

"I shot him, and he went down. Don't know if I killed him," Noah said.

"Hopefully, the river will. Let's go."

"Wait. We need to find him, sir. Get a team and find him. We can't just leave him, especially if he's still alive."

Sheriff Sullivan got right in Noah's face. "I know you have some sort of righteous agenda to fulfill, but this ain't the way, son. If I send men out there to look for some thug who broke my nose, they'll freeze to death, get lost, or die by a man we couldn't stop. Jay Kirk was as forgettable as his father. It's best that he dies on his own, alone, in the cold. We can go looking when the storm lets up. Right now, I'm going to get my nose checked out and go to bed. I suggest you get some rest after you get your arm checked out. Goodnight, Noah."

Sheriff Sullivan got in his car and headed back to the station. Noah would also go back and fill out the mountain of paperwork needed after shooting a suspect. He had mixed feelings about the night since he couldn't find a solution to the trouble with Jay. He hoped that in a few days, once the storm let up, he would find Jay dead. Or in bad enough shape that he could take him into custody without incident.

Jay wouldn't be found in a few days, though. Police and rescue teams would search for a week before giving up and concluding that his body had floated into the bay and become lost.

Jay pulled himself from the river after being caught on a low-hanging branch that prevented him from being swept away. He climbed to snowy land, catching his breath. The bag on his back was soaked through, yet the money remained intact. It would need to dry, as would he. He would need a place to get warm and avoid illness from soaking in the icy water for so long, but at least he wasn't dead. He was motivated. He was ready to take his second chance. It was time to give the Kirk name the reputation it deserved. If the soaking clothes and blood loss didn't kill him by morning, that was.

CHAPTER 2

THE NEW TOWN

Eight years had passed since Officer Noah chased Jay Kirk and lost him in the storm. Now a detective, he had seen plenty of action, but that night still haunted him. He was weeks away from taking over for the soon-to-be-retired Sheriff Sullivan, who basically ran the show. Noah looked forward to taking over and felt even more excited since local crime had dwindled to nearly nothing in the last two years.

The most recent crime that Noah investigated was a string of car break-ins by a couple of teenagers. An embarrassing assignment, to say the least, as he had devoted his life to protecting the law, and now, he was merely stopping crime on a rookie level. Regardless, he was comfortable knowing he wasn't jeopardizing his life every day and could live in a safe town. A town so small that it could only accommodate a few hundred residents.

The town was in the final stages of preparing its annual street fair and would begin the event in the next few days. Noah was on duty to keep an eye out not just for troublesome teenagers but and any strangers rolling into town. The previous year was rumored to have pushed in some drug dealers, but they were never caught. Noah was determined to put the rumor to rest or detain one of them this year.

Sullivan stormed into Noah's office. "You hear anything about the strange car parked by the vacant lot?"

"No, sir. When did it turn up?" Noah asked.

"Michaels just saw it on his patrol. He called it in about ten minutes ago."

"Maybe someone stopped to take a nap? We don't normally get visitors in town.

Sullivan looked over his shoulder to check for anyone in close proximity to the office. He leaned toward Noah when the coast was clear.

"A kid said he saw three men wearing masks outside the car in the middle of the night," he whispered confidentially. "Kid looks out his window and sees this right in our town. I don't know who these assholes think they're trying to scare, but no one's going to spook me in this town, not days before a massive family event. Get down there and see what you can find. Keep this quiet if you can."

Sullivan turned and exited the office.

"Yes, sir," Noah said to his superior's back. He then grabbed his jacket and headed for the entrance to see about the new visitors.

Michaels was still at the scene when Noah arrived. He was always happy to give Noah a hard time whenever they interacted. Noah had a lot of patience, but even Michaels could push his buttons.

"Well, if it isn't the local detective. Tell me, Noah, does your office have those fancy ergonomic chairs? Your posture is great these days," Michaels said, slapping him on the back.

"I try to get a workout every day, Michaels. Keeps me focused and helps the posture. I appreciate the compliment. What do we have here?"

"Car's been sitting here for about twelve hours. I ran the plates. Missing car from a town thirty miles north of here. Kid across the street tells me he saw three masked men in it during the night. I won't know much until I get surveillance from local spots, but even that's a stretch. Not a lot of coverage in a vacant lot."

"How about forensics?" Noah asked.

"You think it's necessary? We're going off a kid's word. Could be in on a prank," Michaels suggested.

"Better safe than sorry. Sullivan doesn't want any theatrics before the fair."

"I think he's just paranoid before retiring. One slip-up, and there goes his pension."

Noah walked around the car and noticed a deep gash. It looked like the vehicle had been slashed with a large blade. Deep into its side, right behind the back tire.

"In case of someone who wants to try something, maybe it's best that we take this seriously." Noah ran his hand across the large gash in the car.

From the nearby tree line, two sets of eyes looked on at Michaels and Noah. One turned to the other.

"We make our premiere in three days," said one of them as he started walking away. The other followed, and together they entered the woods. "Continue with the plan. We must have our new guests in place for the screening."

Later that evening, the town meeting started around seven. Several adults had gathered with plans for the fair that would soon flow several blocks down Main Street. With most of the stands, rides, and events already planned, they closed the last logistical matters before setting up for the big opening day. Frank Lapolla set his papers down at the head of the table. Noah sat while, in turns, Michelle Thomas addressed the catering and Bob O'Connor went over events and activities.

"Okay, we do this thing in four days," Frank said. "Let's try to cover all the bases before the fun starts on Friday. We haven't had any issues in the last several years, so I'm hoping this year runs as smoothly."

"That's because you took over for Derek, Frank. He had no clue how to keep this fair together," Michelle chuckled. She took every opportunity to flirt with Frank once she heard he had separated from his wife. She developed a schoolgirl crush on him after her husband died the year before. She seemed to move on more quickly than most. But she had needs, and something about Frank told her he could fulfill them.

"I appreciate that, Michelle," Frank said. "Derek did a fine job most of the time. The diner fire wasn't really his fault. His reaction was worse than the fire."

A small fire had broken out in the diner just after the lunch rush. Instead of calmly addressing the issue, Derek was quick to yell obscenities at the cook responsible. After several mothers were disgusted to hear a grown man yell foul language in front of their children, Derek was swiftly removed from the following year's planning and replaced by Frank. As a little league coach for ten years, Frank was excellent with children and had no difficulty behaving in front of them.

"Bob, where are we on entertainment?" Frank asked.

"The DJ arrives the night before and will set up early in the morning. The bounce castles for the kids are arriving the afternoon before and will be set up in the morning. I'm waiting on some emails from street performers, but otherwise, we are in good shape," Bob answered.

"Great. How's catering, Michelle?"

"A few restaurants will set up early Friday morning. Food trucks will pull up either Thursday evening or Friday morning and set up to block the cross streets. Once we get plans for the street closures, we'll be in good shape, Frank," Michelle said, tossing her hair from one shoulder to the next in a flirtatious gesture.

Frank didn't pick up on it.

"Excellent. Noah, anything to add before we wrap this up?" Frank asked.

"I don't want to alarm anyone," Noah said, "but Michaels and I spotted a stolen car by the vacant lot. We don't know any details yet, but I'll have more officers out on patrol during the fair. Just a precaution."

"Keep me posted on that. We don't need any spooked residents during our most family-oriented event of the year," Frank added.

"Believe me, I already have Sullivan breathing down my neck about it. He's going to die of stress before he retires," Noah said.

The group laughed at his comment.

"If you guys are good," he continued, "I'm going to take off. I just wanted to share the news."

"We appreciate it, Noah. See you in a few days unless something comes up," Frank said.

Noah waved to the group on his way out. He felt confident that the upcoming fair would lift his spirits from the unusual vacant car that alarmed him earlier today.

Benny Kalfa kept riding back and forth through town on his bike between seeing this and that friend. Each time he passed the vacant lot with the mysterious car, something in his mind told him to stop and investigate.

Throw a rock at the window!

Each time, the voice got a little bit louder. He had ridden by at least four times that day. By the time he was on his way home, it was dark out. He knew his mother might yell at him for being late, but he could talk his way out of getting into serious trouble. When he passed the car that time, he threw his bike down and picked up a rock. He passed it from hand to hand before winding back and tossing it at the unoccupied car in the vacant lot. The first throw flew past the car by a long shot. Had he been with any of his friends, they would've laughed at Benny profusely until their sides hurt or they were lying on the ground.

Benny sighed and grabbed another rock. This one hit the hood dead center. He smiled and reached for another rock. The windshield was the primary target, and he was more confident in his third throw. As he wound back and aimed, he heard a ruffling in the bushes.

"Hey, kid, what the fuck are you doing?" said a voice.

Benny couldn't make out a face or even a figure. He put his arm down and walked toward where he heard the voice.

"Who's that?" he asked. "Who's there?"

"Do you know the owner of that car?" asked the voice.

"No. I heard someone left it here. Probably a drug addict or something," Benny said, winding back for his third and hopeful throw. "No use to anyone in town if it's been here all day."

"Back the fuck away from it," said the voice. "Right now!"

Benny was going to offer the stranger a few obscenities before he heard a faint whisper. It sounded like a few different voices were now engaged in a private conversation.

"Hey, what's your name?" asked a second voice.

This person sounded much more composed and even-tempered, so Benny didn't feel as uncomfortable talking to him.

"Benny. What's yours?"

"Hello, Benny," said the kind voice. "I apologize for my brother's attitude. He can be a little aggressive sometimes. I'm the owner of the car. I'd rather not explain the whole situation right now, but we were accused of something we didn't do, so we're trying to lay low in your lovely town."

"How do I know this is really *your* car?"

"Do you have a lot of people in your town hiding in the trees at night?" the voice asked.

"I guess you have a point. Sorry for throwing rocks at your car." Benny reached for his bike.

"Hold on a second, Benny. Maybe you can help us," said the nice voice. "That is, if you're willing to help a few kind strangers."

"What do you need from me?"

There was no answer for quite some time. For a moment, Benny thought they'd fled. Or maybe they were just a few kids trying to scare him so they could mock him in school the next day. Then the ruffling resumed, reassuring him that he was talking to a vagabond wandering around his town. Within seconds, a rock flew out of the bushes and hit Benny square in the forehead. He dropped to the ground, slamming the back of his head on the pavement. He lay still, trying to compose himself while blood flowed over his eyes from the open gash.

Two shadows stood over Benny. Fading in and out, he struggled to identify them.

"Bullseye!" said the less friendly voice.

"You didn't have to hit him in the face," remarked the kind voice. "We need him alive and well. I don't know if we can get much out of him in this condition."

Now realizing the seemingly trustworthy voice was connected to such cruelty, Benny felt stupid.

"In a few days, it won't matter if he gives us everything we need or one word," said the crueler voice. "Tonight, we start with him."

A silhouette reached down, dragged Benny to the trunk of the car, and popped it open.

"Are you going to help me?" asked the cruel voice.

Benny felt hands around his ankles. The owner of those hands lifted him from the ground and dropped him into the trunk. The lid slammed down on his hand, and he yelled out. They hadn't acknowledged Benny's loud sobbing over his searing pain. As much as the pain in his head throbbed, his hand consumed his attention right now. The trunk closed again, and Benny was left gripping his broken hand as it dripped blood. The scarlet stream flowed along his forearm to his elbow, and the warm sensation only worsened his dread. He wanted his mom. He reached for his phone, but it wasn't there. He must have lost it when he hit the ground. The muffled voices were quiet until they opened the car doors. After Benny heard the engine start, he could only make out a few words over its roar. He shifted several times as the car pulled out of the lot toward an unknown destination.

Though eager to get out of the car as quickly as possible, Benny's head ached terribly. In his current state, he knew he couldn't scream or struggle to get away from two adult men. The loud rumbling of the muffler made it harder for him to hear anything inside the car. The soft red glow of the brake lights let him know these people weren't in a hurry.

They're taking me somewhere close.

He figured he could make a run for it when the car opened. Then he could make his way home…if home wasn't too far away.

He faded in and out as they drove for another ten minutes or so. Then the car came to an abrupt stop.

Benny's vision blurred when they pulled him from the car. The bright high beams made it hard for him to see where he was, but the desolate building indicated that he wasn't close to his house anymore. He heard faint whimpering and saw tear-filled eyes looking down at him as he was dragged across the floor.

A woman groaned loudly.

"Quiet, or you'll end up like the hero over here," said the angry voice.

Benny was dropped beside the man to whom the voice referred.

Benny's vision started to return to normal. And that was when he saw the dislocated jaw dangling from the mangled flesh of Mister Kens, a neighborhood prick he didn't care much for.

Being that close to his freshly killed body afforded him no ease. It sent a wave of fear through his entire body. Goosebumps rose all over his skin.

Benny shot up only to be stopped by the owner of the calmer voice, the one who had dragged him there. He looked up to see a haunting masked figure. A vision blacker and scarier than any nightfall Benny had ever experienced.

"Easy, kid. My brother wants you all to see this is an example of what happens to uncooperative people. I'd rather save the bloodshed for the remainder of our guests, but he gets a little cranky if he can't let that anger out. I assure you we're finished for now." He patted Benny on his shoulder.

Benny could see clearly now. The angrier one, also wearing a black mask, returned from outside.

"Are we fucking ready yet?" he asked.

"I'm going to collect the last one. She requires a bit more chivalry." The calm one walked to the door, pulling down a suit bag that dangled from a hook. "All I ask is that you only scare them. Playtime starts tomorrow."

"It better. I'm not standing around much longer."

The brothers dispersed, and the whimpers started again. People felt fear throughout the room. Each of them hoped they would be the last to go.

CHAPTER 3

THE BOY, THE MESSAGE

Noah walked into the precinct as he did most days—iced coffee slowly melting in his hand, sunglasses dangling from his uniform, and a last-minute check of the various links his friends had sent him. They ranged from game highlights to creepy photos of an unknown woman's cleavage taken from across the bar. This Tuesday morning, upon entering the office, he started his day with the looks of distraught parents.

"Detective, can I have a word?" Officer Magnusson asked.

"Did you let the Kalfas into my office?" Noah asked.

"Yes, I'm sorry. That's part of what I wanted to talk to you about—Benny Kalfa is missing."

"Missing?"

"Never came home last night after talking to his mom. But that's not the worst part."

"What's the worst part?"

"He's only one of five people who didn't come home last night. All were reported missing within the last few hours."

"Jesus. Five people? These aren't local drunks that just found some late booty call?" Noah asked.

"No. We have Lynn Perry. Her daughter was distraught because she always answers the phone at the same time every night. Mark Kens was seen talking to a few out-of-towners before getting into their car. Jess Summerson went out on a date and didn't come home. Lastly, we have Mary Weiss, who went to pick up food for her sons and didn't come home after several hours of not answering. Only reason the Kalfas are in your office is because they just came to report it. I went to see if you'd arrived yet. They followed me in and refused to leave."

"Great. Give me updates on these folks. Anyone else asks you for anything, even Sullivan, tell them I said otherwise. Let's get this figured out right away."

"Yes, sir," Magnusson said, walking away. "Good luck with the Kalfas."

"Thanks." Noah gripped the doorknob, taking a deep breath.

The Kalfas stood as Noah entered the office, dread filling both of their eyes.

"Jane, Tom, what's going on?" Noah asked. He'd known Jane and Tom Kalfa since he was a teenager. Former high school sweethearts, they settled in Hyde Cove after graduation. Besides their regular commute to and from the community college, they never left.

"It's Benny. He never came home last night. I went out looking for him and found his bike this morning." Jane's swollen eyes never left Noah's.

"When did you hear from him last?" Noah asked.

"He texted me around seven, saying he would be staying late at a friend's house. Sometimes he loses track of time while playing video games, so I sat by the phone in case he needed a ride home. I fell asleep, and when I checked his room this morning, he wasn't there. He always calls, even when he knows I'm going to yell at him," Jane insisted.

"Normally," Tom cut in, "we wouldn't let him be out so late, but his friend lives at the end of the next street. He's always good about calling, even if it's not always as timely as we'd like."

"You said you found his bike?"

"Yes, right outside the vacant lot on Luel Ann Drive," Jane answered.

Noah's heart skipped a beat. *The car.* He walked over to the door and closed it.

"Was there a car in the lot when you were there this morning?" Noah inquired.

"No, just Benny's bike," Jane said.

"Jane, are you absolutely sure there wasn't a car there?"

"Yes. Why? Who does it belong to?"

"I'll be right back. We'll get a search team out for Benny right away. Hang tight." Noah exited the room abruptly.

Noah walked up and down the precinct halls to find Michaels. He wasn't at his desk, so Noah figured he was taking his always-extended coffee break. It was a selfish luxury Michaels owed to living in a safe town. Still, Noah felt it wasn't his colleague's best move to brag about such a thing openly. Not to his future boss, at any rate.

He entered the kitchen to see Michaels pouring his large coffee.

"Well, if it isn't Detective Noah. What can I do for you this fine morning, sir?" Michaels uttered sarcastically.

"What happened to the car?" Noah asked. "Did you have it towed?"

"The one in the lot? No. It should still be there. Why?"

"Benny Kalfa went missing this morning. His parents told me they found his bike in the lot, and the car is gone."

Michaels' usual smirk reduced to a blank stare. He was always comfortable coasting around without doing any serious work or getting involved in something that he felt would hurt others. Becoming a police officer wasn't his initial goal when he left high school. After his brother went into law enforcement, he saw some of the perks it offered without considering the responsibility that would fall on his shoulders. Today was the day he realized it would be a true challenge for him.

"Jesus Christ. Any idea what time this was?" Michaels asked.

Noah peeked around the corner to see everyone still walking into the precinct quietly. Noah signaled Michaels to follow him, and they proceeded down the hall.

"Keep this quiet for now," Noah instructed. "See if you can get any security footage from nearby businesses for any leads. We need to find that car and whoever brought it here as quickly as possible. I'm going to assemble a search team so the Kalfas don't lose their minds. Report back whenever you hear anything."

Michaels would normally leave with a smart remark. This time, he felt it wasn't appropriate. "Yes, sir. I'll be in touch."

Noah returned to his office with the intent of calming the Kalfas. Once he could do so, he would try and find Benny.

Benny awoke to blurry vision. He could feel the dried blood on his forehead and down his cheeks. He slowly lifted his concussed head as the dizziness set in immediately. All the people who surrounded him the night before were now gone. Only one woman lay next to him. He noted her blue gown and expensive jewelry, the kind Mom put on when she went out drinking with Dad. Then he remembered one of them mentioning a date. It all made sense. Marring her beauty were heavily blackened eyes and what appeared to be a serious head wound. Dried blood had formed a brownish crust down to her chest. And he wasn't sure if she was alive or dead.

He noticed an uncomfortable presence all around him. He slowly turned to see three masked figures sitting in front of him on a tattered couch. One mask resembled a beast-like character, complete with a splatter of red paint or what Benny hoped wasn't dried blood. Another mask resembled a smiling child-like face. The eyes were the darkest black Benny had ever seen. The third mask in the middle, the most terrifying for Benny, was all white except for black eyes with tiny white dots in the middle.

He shifted in his chair, ready to move his aching body, only to find his wrists bound together behind his back. His legs were tied tightly by the ankles around the legs of the chair.

The beast-masked man pointed at himself. "I'm Brother Berserk."

The man with the smile pointed at himself next. "I'm Brother Ecstatic. Pleased to meet ya!"

The man in the middle stood. "I'm Brother Sight. I apologize for your excessive injuries."

"I don't," Brother Berserk said, interlocking his fingers. "Hell of a good throw if you ask me."

"What do you want with me?" Benny asked.

Brother Sight walked toward Benny and knelt at his feet.

"We want to ask you a few things before we release you," Brother Sight said. "That's all."

"Like what?"

"Who the fuck saw you before we hit you in the lot?" Brother Berserk asked.

"Berserk, please. Let me handle this. Your time will come," Brother Sight said, waving at his impatient brother. He turned back to Benny. "We need to know if anyone else saw you at the lot or knew you were there. Did you tell any of your friends you were going to smash it up the way you did?"

Benny shook his head. "No. I didn't tell anyone."

Brother Ecstatic started to giggle. "I think someone is telling a fib!"

"I'm not. I swear. No one knows," Benny said.

Brother Sight glared at Benny before standing and walking back to his brothers. He looked at both before turning back to look at Benny.

"We believe you. We know you didn't mean to do anything outside of being a kid. All of us would break a car window at your age," Brother Sight said.

"Hell, I lost count of the ones I smashed," Brother Berserk said.

Brother Sight pointed at his courageous brother. "See what I mean?"

Benny smiled and exhaled deeply. He was anxious around the masked brothers but felt slightly at ease, knowing they understood his position.

"However, fate brought us together last night," Brother Sight continued. "You're just a kid. People love kids. Your parents are probably worried sick. But you have been chosen for us. We were once residents of this small town. Horrible things were done to our family name, and we're here to drag it out of the mud. People will remember us for the rest of their lives."

"*The rest of their lives.* That's a great one, brother!" Brother Ecstatic yelled before leaning back in his seat and howling with laughter.

"Please don't hurt me. I'm sorry I damaged your car. Please," Benny said while tears formed in his eyes. "I won't tell anyone."

"That's what we're counting on, kid," Brother Berserk said. He stood, drawing a knife from his boot. He stepped away from the couch and stood next to Brother Sight. "Is it time?"

"It's time," Brother Sight said, walking behind Benny. He positioned himself there and untied his restraints.

Benny immediately pulled his wrists in front of his chest, touching each one gently to feel the irritable burns left by the rope.

"I give you my word that I won't—" Benny's plea became a gasp when the knife sank deep into his side. With shock, confusion, and terror, he looked into the soulless eyes of Brother Berserk, who stood in front of him, gripping the knife. Tears fell down his face as his last moments of life overwhelmed him.

Brother Berserk dragged the blade in one swift motion, opening Benny's stomach like a torn garbage bag. Blood and intestines released onto the floor, and Brother Berserk could feel the warmth escape Benny's body.

Benny's head went limp as life fleeted.

"I don't know why we didn't start with that," Brother Berserk said, wiping his blood-slickened knife on his jeans. He returned the blade to his boot. "We don't need theatrics. That's wasting time."

"It sends a message. If we start with a full-on assault, we're not going to get our point across. We do this for our name, not for the body count," Brother Sight said.

Brother Sight approached Benny, gently sliding his fingers through the tangled, syrupy-textured hair.

"He'll be a fine little messenger," Brother Sight said, smiling. "Ecstatic, did you find a good spot for him?"

Brother Ecstatic chuckled, covering his mouth to keep his laughter from provoking Brother Berserk's temper. He cleared his throat and stepped toward Brother Sight.

"Yes, I know just the spot! You guys up for putting him in the trunk for me? Pretty please?" Brother Ecstatic chuckled.

A few minutes later, Brother Ecstatic drove away from the vacant building while Brother Sight removed the rope from the bloody chair.

"Are you sure the stream is going to work? I want them all to see their families ripped apart," Brother Berserk said.

Brother Sight placed his hand on Brother Berserk's shoulder. "Brother, your anger is a quality I admire. But too much of it will be your downfall. Trust in our efforts. Hyde Cove is days away from remembering us forever."

CHAPTER 4

THE FUN STARTS

Friday morning came, and the town was still. Noah's car sat at the corner of Main and Cherry. He walked toward the tents, sipping his coffee. He peered around at the crews. Some set up food and game stations while others inflated bounce houses for the kids and intoxicated adults who felt daring. He approached Frank, who stood by the catering tents with a well-organized pile of papers on his clipboard.

"Detective, the fun doesn't start for a few more hours," Frank said, grinning. "I can get you to the front of the line for the bounce castle, but anything else will make people think I'm favoring you."

Noah smirked. "I'll settle for some funnel cake. How's everything running?"

"A few people running late. But nothing to worry about. Any news on the vacant car?"

"It's gone. We think whoever passed through took it and left. I'll still have additional officers because we got word of a missing boy. Just in case."

"Missing boy? Who?"

Noah looked around before leaning in toward Frank. "Benny Kalfa."

"Really? When was this?" Frank asked.

"We're still investigating. I don't want to spook anyone before we know anything. Just give me some extra space near the cross streets to position additional officers this evening," Noah said. "I'll be back in a little while to discuss details."

Noah looked up the street and saw Michaels exiting his car.

Michaels nodded at Noah, lacking the usual sarcastic demeanor he often displayed around his colleagues.

"Excuse me, Frank." Noah patted Frank on the shoulder before walking to Michaels.

"Good morning, Detective," Michaels said.

"Any leads on the Kalfa kid or the car?" Noah asked.

"Yes and no," Michaels answered. "We've confirmed that two suspects attacked and kidnapped Benny in the same car that was left in the lot. No leads since we don't think these two are from around here. We have Benny, the two perps, and the suspicious car on one security tape. We find the car, and we find all three."

"Okay. Keep working on it. I'll be down at the station in about an hour. Also, see how many officers we can spare tonight?"

"For what?" Michaels asked.

"I'd rather have reinforcements. Just in case someone tries something stupid while the citizens of our town are all in one place together.

Michaels nodded and then returned to his car. Once behind the wheel, he headed to the station.

Noah consulted his watch and decided to patrol the outskirts of town for any signs of trouble. He had the time even though he had already told Michaels he'd get to the station in an hour. He felt it was necessary for his own peace of mind if things went the way his ominous thoughts were leading. He headed to the bridge that rested on the edge of town. He hadn't been there much since shooting Jay Kirk all those years ago. But it was another way for drifters and vagabonds to come and go, so he wanted to see for himself.

Noah arrived at the bridge. The breeze brushed against his face as he exited the car. Some of the shingles on the covered bridge roof dangled from the side—the result of years of poor maintenance. Noah had been an advocate for getting it repaired for many years, but no one else on the board wanted to prioritize such a project. Despite being a favored route for traveling, it slowly rotted away on the edge of town. Noah walked onto the bridge, leaning against the railing to admire the water below. He heard birds chirping and spotted the occasional small deer going about its instinctual habits beneath him.

The bridge was peaceful. He couldn't remember the last time he had a moment like this to himself. Maybe three years. His fiancé, Cindy, called off their engagement years ago after he couldn't devote sufficient time to her. He had wanted to be a detective so badly that he sacrificed all his free time to that goal. He got it at the cost of his love life. He wanted to make amends with Cindy after he achieved the promotion. When that happened, he could entreat her to see he could be the man

41

she needed, that he could now give her exactly what she wanted.

She was killed in a car accident two days before they were supposed to meet. Despite all his efforts, Noah knew she had died without clarity, which had haunted him ever since. He did his best to devote his time to being an honest man and detective of integrity. He owed her that much after not letting himself make her a priority. The bridge was one of her favorite spots in town to stroll by, so he spent some time there to reflect on her.

Noah stood by the bridge for a while and then walked toward the other side. He got to the opposite railing from where his car was parked and looked around for a little while.

The smell hit him right away.

It was faint but the scent wafted toward him like a speeding car when the wind blew. He gagged and looked around, covering his nose as he walked. He looked over the railing and saw a shoe dangling just under the bridge.

He climbed over the railing and slowly descended the bank of the river. He held on to a thick bush as the steep hill provided little balance from falling into the water. He held tightly and looked up to see the horror of what remained of Benny Kalfa. He hung by his neck from a thick rope, swaying slowly. Both of his shoes were untied and barely on his feet. A large gash in his stomach exposed his intestines as they dangled from his torn shirt. His pants were soaked and reeked of his final excremental purge. His eyes were still slightly open, their gaze directed at the babbling river.

Noah carefully walked closer to stand steadily under the bridge where the ground provided more flat space. He stared up at Benny, examining every grotesque detail. He noted the dried blood on Benny's face while trying not to imagine the horrors he faced in his last moments. *How am I going to tell his parents? How does this happen in such a quiet town?* Noah's thoughts didn't slow. Instead, he sought to absorb every detail that might give him a clue as to who'd done this.

It was barely noticeable, but Noah saw a piece of paper loosely stuffed in Benny's pocket. He couldn't reach it since Benny was nearly another foot above Noah's head. He searched for a large branch and, against all standard procedure, gently pushed the paper free. Noah's gut told him the words on that page were intended to be read immediately. It took some patience, but the paper slowly fell to Noah. He grabbed it, reading it right away. There were very few things in the world that stunned Noah to his core: not settling his past with Cindy, some of his abusive memories of his mother, and the occasional outbursts from Sheriff Sullivan when he was a rookie. The words on the paper dwarfed all of those.

NOW TWO LIE STILL BENEATH THIS BRIDGE.

Noah knew instantly that the note's author had penned it in reference not only to Benny but also Jay Kirk. After all these years, someone still had it out for him for what happened. It also stunned him that someone else knew about him after so long. He climbed up the hill again and made his way to his car. He pulled out his phone and dialed quickly.

"Michaels, I found Benny Kalfa at the bridge. We're going to have a long night ahead of us. Get Sullivan down here right away," Noah said before hanging up the phone. He reread the note over and over until he heard the sirens in the distance.

Police were able to get Benny Kalfa down within thirty minutes. The entire bridge was taped off as Michaels, Sullivan, and Noah stood off to the side, all while crime scene investigators examined the scene and bagged the note Noah had found.

"It doesn't make any fucking sense. Other than his aunt, who died years ago, no one else gave a shit about him," Sullivan said.

"Didn't he have any younger siblings?" Noah asked.

"They were in foster care right after their aunt died," Sullivan said. "Twin brothers and another older one. The oldest was only twelve or so. I doubt he knew what his brother was up to at such an age."

Noah paced back and forth. "Can we get access to their files?"

"I'll give it a try. It might be hard since we don't know if they're even involved," Sullivan said.

"I can look into any relatives we may not know about. Distant cousins, abusive ex-girlfriend, people like that," Michaels said.

Noah nodded. He figured the brothers were a stretch, but someone knew how Jay had died. He didn't want that old case to be responsible for other people getting hurt.

"Maybe we should cancel the fair…just to be safe," Noah said. "The whole town is going to be vulnerable."

"Absolutely not," Sullivan snapped. "We've already invested too much time and money into this. It's our annual event for the entire town. People look forward to this all year. As horrible as this is, we can't let low spirits ruin this fair. Have extra men set up roadblocks. And keep this quiet. I'll make an official announcement when the time is right." He headed for his car after signaling to a few officers standing by.

Noah and Michaels stared at one another, trying to process the facts. The man they formally looked up to had just told them to have a celebration instead of mourning the loss of a murdered local boy. On top of that, he would retreat to his office to ride out the remainder of his time before retirement rather than contribute to his community. Though Sullivan valued the money that would pour into the businesses—vendors in whose establishments he regularly stuffed his face—Noah and Michaels knew he would avoid much of the fair.

"What do we do?" Michaels asked.

"I'm going to go to the Kalfas myself. Look into anyone else who may be connected to Jay Kirk. Distant relatives, ex-girlfriends, whatever. I want to make an arrest before the fair is over."

"Yes, sir," Michaels said.

The two went their separate ways.

Noah had never looked a parent in the eyes and told them their child had been ripped open like a wild animal. Even though he was attending with hundreds of smiling faces, he wouldn't have an ounce of fun at the fair all weekend.

In the distance, Brother Ecstatic looked upon the police activity from the trees. He giggled to himself. Then he raced back to the discreet location where he and his brothers prepared the next horrific phase of their revenge against Hyde Cove.

CHAPTER 5

FAMILY REUNITED

The evening came, and residents of Hyde Cove flooded into the Main Street fair like a swarm of ants consuming dropped food. Parents, still exhausted from their workday, chased kids and swallowed down food that satisfied their lack of desire to cook. Kids piled into the bounce castles, and restaurants formed lines outside.

At least twenty officers, Noah included, watched the festivities, closely observing everyone at the event. Many families took the time to speak to the officers and thanked them for standing close by. Most of the officers reciprocated with smiles and handshakes. Noah stood further back, still at a loss for words after telling the Kalfas their son had been murdered.

Upon hearing the heartbreaking news, Jane Kalfa immediately collapsed. Tom Kalfa held his wife tightly on the floor, hysterically crying before she even shed a single tear. Noah offered his condolences, but it was as helpful as a Band-Aid on shattered bone. Their beloved son had seen his last moments in the most brutal way possible, and they'd have to go on without him. Noah offered them counseling and closure by assuring them the person responsible would be brought to justice. They didn't even hear Noah's words, so he politely left after the horrendous news left his lips.

All of the officers were sworn to secrecy until the fair was over. Gossip of a boy killed that very same morning was enough to tear apart the community, so there were hopes they could keep the spirit alive while the town was distracted. Despite the people still missing, Noah made sure it was a top priority at the station to keep him informed as he watched closely at the fair. He checked his phone every few minutes, worrying he'd miss an update.

Noah raised the walkie-talkie to his mouth. "Keep a sharp eye out, men. Anything unusual pops up, you report to me immediately."

"Once that pie-eating contest gets rolling, I think we'll have some unusual sights," Officer Stahli said over the walkie.

"Especially if Ian Ross is competing again this year. He'll probably finish the pies the losers can't finish," Officer Melville chuckled.

Noah grew irritated, but not as quickly as Michaels. "Both of you shut the fuck up. Last I checked, neither of you has seen below your bellies in at least ten years. A boy is dead, and you're making jokes? Fucking disgusting."

The radio chatter came to a halt.

Noah was impressed with Michaels' ability to maintain professionalism. They kept their eyes open and saw nothing out of the ordinary for quite some time. The families were all enjoying the fair as much as expected. Adults stuffed their faces with mounds of French fries and

48

funnel cake. Kids ran from bounce castle to bounce castle and on to some of the rides while their parents pulled out stacks of tickets to exchange for more time on the rides. Teenagers flocked to the games to win stuffed animals for themselves and their friends, some bulky enough to make carrying them difficult.

Noah couldn't help but smile when he noticed all the excitement. He was proud of his little town and nearly ridding the people of threats on a daily basis. Even though the image of Benny Kalfa was burned in the back of his mind forever, he still felt he had won over his fellow citizens. Despite whoever was connected to this through Jay Kirk, the real criminals were long gone. The real crimes had been settled years ago. But crime had resurfaced again in Hyde Cove—a senseless, grisly crime that would shake the community for some time.

Sullivan arrived at the fair, walking with a few officers. He got to the stage in the center of the fair and strolled up as if the event's purpose was to honor him.

"Heads up. Someone's about to steal all of our glory," Noah chuckled.

Some of the other officers looked at him, smiling. They stayed quiet as Sullivan tapped the microphone, blasting out a piercing ring that caught the attention of everyone present.

"Hello. Hello. Good evening, everyone. I hope you're all enjoying our annual fair," Sullivan said, followed by a burst of applause. He always liked to give a speech on Friday night to look good in front of the community, even though everyone knew he hadn't done much in his last six months of duty. "I wish you all a fun-filled weekend and hope to see your smiling faces until we wrap up on Sunday evening. Now, there's one announcement I'd like to make before I send you all back to the fun."

Noah exchanged glances with some of the other officers, followed by rolling their eyes. Sullivan couldn't take five minutes to talk to fellow officers unless he needed something but would talk for an hour if it meant improving his reputation. Noah couldn't bear another 'I love my community' speech without tossing up fried Oreos.

"I'm retiring at the end of summer. After thirty long years on duty, I'm ready to pass the torch to the next qualified person to ensure the community is safe, looked after, and properly steered toward a better future. That's why, effective immediately, I am promoting Detective Maxwell Noah to Lieutenant as I begin delegating my responsibilities elsewhere. Are you out there, Detective? Come and give us some kind words." Sullivan stepped away from the microphone. He started applauding, inspiring a thunderous response from the crowd.

Noah slowly approached the stage and tried not to blush as he was cheered on. Once there, he met Sullivan's eyes and firmly gripped his hand in a celebratory shake.

"You've earned it. I mean it," Sullivan whispered.

Noah looked out at the crowd to see smiling faces and a welcoming community looking back at him. He approached the mic. He struggled to find the words to say since he hadn't expected this in any regard.

"First off, I'd like to thank Chief Sullivan for the honor. This wasn't expected at all, but I'm flattered that he feels I'm the man for the job. Truthfully, I've never seen any other path for myself besides protecting the community and people who make me feel at home."

As the words escaped him, Cindy's face popped into Noah's head. He remembered the numerous fights, canceled dates, and ultimatum she gave him for not giving her the attention she needed. It was always his dedication to the force, pursuing criminals, and becoming a better officer. The memory of her tears made the words flee from his brain. He could hear Sullivan clearing his throat multiple times, trying to get him to continue.

Noah saw the wandering eyes, and he returned to the present. He peered over at Sullivan. "Sorry, I lost my train of thought."

He returned his attention to the crowd.

"I give you my word that I'll do my best to be honest and loyal to all of you, to serve this town, and to offer the protection it deserves. Thank you for this. And let's have a great time this weekend." Noah stepped away from the mic and enjoyed the applause that followed his words. He gave Sullivan another handshake and made his way back to his post.

Noah walked off with a new attitude for the evening. The Kalfa boy took a back seat while his career goals were driving full speed. He was getting closer to the dream of being a respected law enforcer and was surrounded by dozens of people who celebrated with him. Thoughts of his dream coming along filled his mind until

51

the blaring sound of static came from the local electronics store.

People went quiet as the amplified sound shot from speakers in the front window, and the monitors synced together to show the video static. The screen went black and then displayed the three brothers sitting on the couch that Benny Kalfa saw upon waking in their hideout.

Noah raised the walkie-talkie to his lips. "Heads up," he whispered. "Got something at the electronics store."

The three masked brothers sat there quietly for a moment as the town's people looked on. The music turned off, and people stopped running around and conversing to focus on the bizarre image. Sullivan stared with horrified confusion in his eyes.

"Good evening, people of Hyde Cove," Brother Sight said. "Are you all enjoying your evening? We're certainly about to. Tonight is a very special night for all of us. First, let's all congratulate Officer Noah on his promotion again." He leaned toward the camera. "That's right. We can see and hear all of you."

"We're going to keep this short and sweet," Brother Berserk informed them. "We're here to bring back the Kirk name and reclaim Hyde Cove. You imprisoned our father and murdered our brother. We deserve retribution!"

"So many people to play with! *Ee-hehe*! I can't tell you how excited I am!" Brother Ecstatic exclaimed.

Brother Sight stood and picked up the camera while still looking into the lens.

52

"I'll make this easy for everyone. If Police Chief Sullivan and Lieutenant Noah step forward to surrender, we will only do minimal damage. If you're really committed to protecting these people, you will come to us without resistance."

Noah peered at Sullivan, who was drenched in sweat, eyes gleaming with fear. He returned his attention to the monitors.

"How exactly do you expect us to go along with something like that?" Noah asked.

"Keep in mind, Lieutenant, I said minimal damage with your cooperation. Mark my words; the body count is your decision," Brother Sight said. "You already know we're capable of killing one of your townspeople. Don't think we'll hesitate for another one."

"What's he talking about? Did they kill Benny Kalfa?" Frank Lapolla asked.

Faint chatter surrounded Noah, who suddenly felt like a cornered, wounded animal. He tried glancing up at Sullivan, who made no effort to return his troubled stare.

Brother Berserk rose from his seat, gesturing to himself. "The boy was my fine work. This one over here was the one who strung him up." He pointed at Brother Ecstatic.

"As I said before," Brother Sight cut in, "two people can save this town from utter destruction. Otherwise, have fun trying to stop us before more people lose their lives."

Noah felt their threat wasn't as dangerous as they made it seem. Sure, Benny Kalfa had died at their hands.

He'd been riding his bike late at night and was scooped up by them. Half of the police force had attended the fair in an official capacity and were witnesses to the unexpected broadcast. So, he had a feeling their plan would backfire. Noah already had plans in mind for finding these three before the video was over. He smiled and shook his head.

"As amusing as your little threat is," Noah said confidently, "we are more than capable of stopping a few low lives who want to threaten us. I call your bluff and look forward to arresting you while this community safely rests in their homes."

Brother Sight shook his head and returned the camera to its original resting place. He sits down with his brothers, facing the camera.

"Hopefully, we've added something extra to the festivities. Lieutenant, make sure you keep your walkie handy. We'll be in touch. See you soon," Brother Sight said before flicking a small remote at the camera.

The screen went black, and the speakers fell silent. Noah stared back at his reflection before turning to face the troubled people of Hyde Cove. He looked around at the many concerned faces looking at him. He was at a loss for what to do at that moment. He opened his mouth to speak.

"Surely, someone decided to throw a wrench in our annual fun!" Sullivan said, shooting Noah a chiding look. "Not to worry, our new Lieutenant and the officers will look into this matter immediately. Why don't you all return to the fair? We will take care of this."

Faint chatter then erupted into a chorus of outrage. Food and bottles were thrown as the angry crowd piled closer to the stage. Sullivan ducked and dodged as objects flew past his head.

"Someone killed that boy, and we are just now finding out about it?" Frank Lapolla said, cornering Noah against a storefront entrance.

"I needed to keep it quiet while we continued the investigation. We had to think about the well-being of the people in this town," Noah scolded.

Before Frank could continue screaming at Noah, he looked past the gathering crowd to see Michelle Thomas approaching. Her face was ghostly white, and blood leaked from the corner of her mouth. She was within reaching distance when she fell into his arms.

"Michelle, what happened?" Frank asked. "What's wrong?"

Michelle gasped for air. Her eyes sank deeper into her head while blood flowed from each nostril. "They can't keep eating the food." Michelle's arms went limp, and Frank slowly placed her on the ground.

Noah looked up when he heard a series of thuds, only to realize that roughly twenty people had collapsed. All looked to be in the same condition as poor Michelle.

The crowd went silent again.

CHAPTER 6

FIRST WAVE

Noah's ears rang as families swarmed their dying family members, screaming. Children and adults lay on the floor, pale as ghosts, dripping blood from their eyes and noses.

They can't keep eating the food.

He looked for Sullivan, who was nowhere in sight.

"Michaels, get emergency services here immediately. Get the available officers in front of all food service stations," Noah commanded. "Now!"

"What's happening?" Michaels asked.

"Those assholes poisoned the food."

They can't keep eating the food.

The words wouldn't stop playing in Noah's head. He rushed to the food stations, and the servers stood back in frantic retreat.

"No one eats anything for the rest of the night. This food might be contaminated." Noah stormed off, passing a few grieving family members to alert more police officers. "Get as many officers as possible and instruct them to escort families to their vehicles. Tell them to get out of here. We're going to need the space for emergency vehicles passing through. Go."

Within an hour, Noah and paramedics rounded up thirty dead bodies and got them into the ambulances to be sorted at the morgue. Police had every corner and cross street covered for four blocks in either direction. Noah made eye contact with family members that were either hysterical or glaring at him for what they believed was his fault.

They can't keep eating the food.

Benny Kalfa's grisly death had caused Noah's ease to go asunder as quickly as Michelle's body had gone limp. He now knew who had killed Benny and strung him up. The plan was to find them now.

"Michaels, do you have eyes on Sullivan?" he asked.

"Haven't seen him since the video feed went off. I think he was more spooked than some of the kids who had to see that," Michaels said. "Way ahead of you. I'm heading to the station to get any info I can on the Kirk brothers. Fair to say it's them."

"I'll be down once we close everything up here. I'm setting a curfew effective immediately. We're working around the clock until we find these guys," Noah said.

Micheals let out a deep sigh. "Damn, I was really looking forward to a pleasant celebration this year."

"Maybe next year," Noah said.

When the last resident drove off an hour and a half later, the police gathered in a small huddle to speak with Noah.

Berserk looked on from a parked car two blocks away.

"We have most of the force here. Shall I proceed?" he said into his walkie-talkie.

"Negative," Sight responded from his end. "Can't risk it right now. They know we're a threat. Let's pace ourselves. We have yet to show Noah what we did with our other guests."

Berserk rolled his eyes and started the car. "Copy." He drove back toward their hideout, fading into the darkness that consumed the outskirts of Hyde Cove.

Noah faced the officers, who had gathered in a small group. "Tonight, we're faced with a threat way beyond what we've ever seen. We're going to hold a briefing back at the station this evening. We need to find these guys before the week starts."

"Do you think that's possible, Lieutenant?" Officer Melville asked. "I mean, they killed thirty people right under our noses. Who knows who else ate what killed them."

Noah was just as unsure as the nervous officers who stared back at him. He had only one lead on the suspects; they were the younger brothers of Jay Kirk. How they knew what had happened or how they had developed this grand plan remained beyond his immediate knowledge. His plan for the moment was to bide for time.

"Melville, Magnusson, head over to the hospital. Get a feel for what happened to everyone and see if others went there on their own. We'll have to wait until autopsies begin to get anything solid. Take two squad cars to cover more ground. If you see anything at all, call it in, and we'll respond in force. The rest of us are heading back to the station for the game plan," Noah said. A simple nod was all it took for the other officers to fall in line, report back to their cars, and head out.

Despite a night of sheer terror and agony, Noah was pleased with the assured confidence his officers had in him. That's all he had to go on while he closed his car door and drove to the station.

Magnusson drove slowly, eyeing the streets for possible activity to alert him. He wasn't too keen on being out by himself. He wanted to get to the hospital fast and stay there for the remainder of the night. He admittedly wasn't the bravest on the force but took it upon himself to stay strong and reassure himself his .38 would come in handy if someone decided to try anything.

His phone rang. "What is it, Melville?"

"Good. Didn't want you calling me over the radio. Where are you?"

"Seven minutes away from the hospital. You there already?" Magnusson asked.

"Why don't we take a little detour? I think I know where those cocksuckers are. We can corner them and have them surrounded in minutes. Town hero-type shit. We deserve it, don't you think?"

Melville thrived on getting recognition even for the most minor achievement. Magnusson, however, didn't expect a heroic gesture for simply doing his job. Moreover, he still didn't think anyone on the force was ready for the Kirk brothers.

"What the fuck are you talking about? Detour where?" he asked.

"The old steel mill on the edge of town. If I were a psycho killer, I'd be hiding out there," Melville explained.

"We have strict orders. We need to ensure those people at the hospital aren't falling into a trap."

"Wouldn't you rather win the approval of hundreds of townsfolk and get this shit over in an hour or two?" Melville was itching to use his firearm again after an encounter with Jerrod Kirk years ago. He regretted missing the opportunity to gun him down personally. He felt confident that if he were present during the arrest, he could make things go in his favor.

Magnusson guessed he'd be dying to stir up some action to make up for the lack of it all these years.

"Noah would flip his lid if you tried something that stupid," Magnusson said. "Besides, we're still outnumbered. Two against three."

"I've got the shotgun and a box of shells. They won't know what hit them."

"Melville, turn around before you get yourself into more trouble. I'll need you at the hospital."

Melville was quiet, causing Magnusson to worry more than he needed to at the moment.

"Did you hear me, Melville?"

"Yeah. I heard you. Last chance. Heroes or babysitters. Your choice." Melville's tone shifted.

Magnusson didn't want to stir up more trouble than it was worth.

"Hospital. Final decision. Where are you?" he asked.

"Outside of the steel mill already. If I get them, no credit for you. Over and out." Melville hung up, leaving Magnusson unable to respond.

"Melville? Melville! Goddamnit."

Magnusson clicked his lights on and sped toward the hospital. He planned to check in and then call Noah to inform him about Melville. Hopefully, there was a chance Melville would be walking into nothing, and not what Magnusson's gut was telling him.

CHAPTER 7

PARTY CRASHERS

Devan and Rich stood by the front door as more kids piled into the house. They exchanged glances with each girl they eyed from head to toe.

"Ladies, welcome," Devan said. "Drinks in the living room; pizzas and wings in the kitchen. Make yourselves at home."

Without thinking it through, Devan and Rich took it upon themselves to send a mass text to their closest friends. It invited them to gather at Devan's house despite the murders and the continued threat hanging over their town. Luckily, Devan's parents were out of town for the weekend. Giving them a venue for an "end of the world" party. He wasn't sure if anyone other than Rich, the son of a violent and neglectful alcoholic, would attend the party. Clearly, other people had the same idea. Upon entering the house, most claimed word of sneaking out or just not going home after the fair had inspired them to show.

"Hey, do you think this will get broken up with everything going on?" Rich asked.

"Please. Everyone's car is in the backyard, and the cops have their hands full. I wouldn't sweat it. My parents can't yell at me until Monday evening, so I'll figure it out then," Devan said before drinking his beer down and proceeding to the kitchen.

Rich looked out the front window briefly while drinking his beer. For a moment, he thought he saw someone staring at him through the trees. He opened the front door to get a better look, but no one was there. He swung the door closed and rejoined the party.

Sight held Ecstatic's chest for a beat before dropping his arm and setting him loose. He let out a sigh. "I told you. Subtle, little brother. We don't want to spook anyone before we terrify them."

"*HE-HEHE*! Sorry, big brother!" Ecstatic said. "I just get so excited!"

"Jesus Christ, keep it down, for fuck's sake," Berserk spat.

Sight poked his blade against Berserk's gut. "Relax. You know he doesn't know any better."

Berserk dropped his head. His frustrations about Ecstatic's mental limitations made it hard for him to concentrate sometimes. Though forced to control his anger a little more when they were together, he still loved his brother. He valued keeping the family name intact as much as Sight did.

"The police are figuring out our real identities by now. We have a tight window, but that doesn't mean we can't have some fun first," Sight said.

Sight, standing five inches taller than his younger twin brothers, gave a confident nod to both of them. They simultaneously drew their knives and walked toward the house, splitting up in different directions.

Devan chuckled as he led Courtney up the stairs. She'd been his crush ever since she told one of their teachers to go fuck herself during an assembly. Despite having the biggest breasts in school, he was mostly drawn to her daring behavior, which was natural to his character. They had both pounded several drinks, and Courtney fixed Devan with a seductive stare he'd always hoped to see.

"It was so great of you to throw a party to lift everyone's spirits," she said.

"I wanted to," Devan said. "Sure, this town is a mess right now, but we only have a short time here, and I want to enjoy it." His hands slid around Courtney's waist and rested on her lower back.

"I should probably thank you for your hospitality."

Courtney grabbed Devan's hand from behind her back and moved it over her breasts. She squeezed his hand against them before reaching up to kiss him. Devan wrapped his other arm around her waist while occupying her bust. He pulled her into his room. They kissed each other with intensity, falling onto his bed. Courtney pulled her shirt over her head, revealing an eyeful for Devan. The guys in the locker room frequently talked about the very position he was in right now. Devan was pleasantly surprised that, without her shirt on, Courtney was way better than fantasy. He kissed her more while tugging at her clasps.

Creaking steps echoed from the next room. Courtney stopped Devan's advances for fear of being revealed to someone other than him. Despite her bravery in standing up to school faculty, she maintained a discreet sexual reputation even with everyone talking about her chest all day.

"What was that?" Courtney asked. "Is someone else up here?"

"It's nothing. Don't you worry," Devan said while kissing Courtney's neck, "my house just creaks."

Courtney pushed Devan off. "Can you go check it out? It sounded like footsteps."

"Courtney, no one else is up here. I promise you," Devan insisted.

"I'm not risking one of your pervert friends seeing me fuck you. Would you please go look?" Courtney said, her level of insistence trumping his.

Devan rolled his eyes and stood up. He walked to the door and looked down the hallway to see a dark, empty view. He turned back to Courtney, still in awe of how far he'd already gotten with her. She pointed to the wall separating Devan's room from the main bedroom, telling Devan to proceed. The darkness in the bedroom proved almost as intense as the hallway, and the streetlights' dim glow from outside cast a shadow of the blinds on the wall opposite Devan. Too lazy and tipsy to find the light switch, he gave the room a cursory glance before turning to exit. After all, it was time to earn those bragging rights among his friends.

Then another creak sounded, this one louder than the last, and echoed around the empty room.

Devan looked back and scanned the whole room from the doorway. The closet door groaned open to reveal light reflecting off of something he couldn't identify. He walked closer until he heard a faint chuckle.

"Rich, if you fuck this up for me, I'm gonna slit your throat," Devan said accusingly as he charged the closet door.

He opened the door to stare into blackness, and the laughter came again, slightly louder. Devan was irritated, growing mad. He wanted to unleash his anger, but he stopped when he noticed the quick blur of movement, a fraction of a second before his mouth filled with blood. His throat burned while he tried to draw air, but nothing filled his lungs but warm fluid. Devan reached up to touch an open wound that drenched his hands in blood.

Ecstatic stepped out of the closet, covering his mouth from expelling too much laughter. "Looks like I'll be doing the throat-slitting tonight. *He-hehe!*" he chuckled through his fingers.

Devan dropped to the carpeted floor. He tried to yell for Courtney, but he could barely make more than a gurgling sound.

Ecstatic sat on Devan's torso and put the knife to his chest. "Now, let's play some more," he said.

Devan would only be alive for another minute or so, but he was forced to watch this masked man slide the knife in and out of his chest. He struggled to breathe as crimson fluid his mouth and overwhelmed his lungs.

Even with Devan's body lying still, Ecstatic continued his knife play, giggling all the while.

Courtney lay impatiently on the bed, waiting for Devan. She clicked her phone on to glance at her notifications and quickly turned it off. She sat up and looked at the open door, expecting Devan's return. Not seeing him, she stood up, irritated.

"Devan. Is everything okay?" she asked.

Courtney heard chuckling coming from the hallway. She took a step back, fearful of a prank. Nor did she want someone to bust in and see her topless. Devan's head crept into the doorway.

"Asshole, you scared the crap out of me. Get in—" Courtney started before noticing his unusual expression.

Devan's severed head dropped into the room and bounced toward her. It stopped and fell on its side, facing her feet. She stared at it, unable to process what was happening. She looked at her feet and noticed the blood splatter. She tried screaming but immediately felt a knife dig deep into her side.

Ecstatic, already covered in Devan's blood, retracted the knife and sprayed Devan's floor with Courtney's.

She gripped her side, holding the wound as wetness flowed down her side and soaked into her jeans. She stumbled back, falling onto the bed.

"Geez, you are very pretty. Did I spoil your fun with lover boy?" Ecstatic gently kicked Devan's head.

Courtney put her hand in front of her face as if it would protect her. Ecstatic crept toward her slowly, appreciating the time he had with her. The faint chuckling under his mask was what upset Courtney the most. She was brave, but all the worst ways of dying immediately popped into her head. Somehow, drowning or getting eaten alive by a wild animal seemed more appealing to her at this very moment. She was seconds away from the end, her heart beating in terror.

Ecstatic swung the blade, ripping into her stomach just above the belly button. The intensity drove the knife so deep that half the handle disappeared into the gaping wound. She groaned as blood dripped from the corners of her mouth. Tears filled her eyes. She reached up to grip the mask.

"Please!" Courtney cried out. "Please stop!"

Ecstatic drove the knife into her stomach again, slightly higher this time. He twisted the handle, watching the dying teen struggle more as he applied pressure to the gaping wound.

"I don't want to—"

Ecstatic plunged his knife into Courtney's eye, killing her instantly. He tried pulling it out, but it was stuck.

"Geez, sometimes I don't know my own strength," Ecstatic commented on his work. He pulled Courtney from the bed by her feet, dragging her into the hallway. He paused at the top of the stairs to see someone slowly coming up.

"Yeah, yeah. I know. Let me go ask Devan," Rich said. He looked upstairs to see darkness.

"Hey, Devan, you getting your dick sucked, or can I talk to you?"

Rich looked down the hall to see darkness. He peeked into Devan's bedroom. As far as he could tell, it was empty. A dark stain on the floor caught his attention, but he couldn't make out what it was.

"Listen, dude, I'm way too high to play hide-and-seek right now. Can you just let me know where you stashed the rest of your blunt wraps? We're trying to smoke up some more in the backyard."

A loud thud came from behind him. He turned to see Courtney's corpse fall from the closet to the floor. Rich looked up to see Ecstatic stepping out after her.

"You can never keep a good grip on a dead body. Am I right?" Ecstatic said, advancing on Rich.

Rich screamed and ran from the room, stumbling down the stairs. Several people at the party stopped to see what the noise was about. People gathered by the door and looked up at Rich coming down in a panic.

"We have to leave," Rich yelled. "Everyone, we have to leave!"

"Chill the fuck out, Rich. See a ghost or something?" Gabe asked.

Normally known as a bully in school, Gabe stood around socializing with several kids. They likely talked to him out of fear. Still, it seemed a perfect time to collect dirt on him in exchange for his cessation of ill-treatment. Rich, however, was never one to be intimidated by him.

"Gabe, I'm serious. We—" Rich started.

He went quiet when he saw the body drop from the staircase to the floor. Courtney's corpse banged to the ground, spraying Gabe and Rich with her blood. The knife pushed deeper into her when she landed on her face, piercing flesh and bone to jut from the back of her head. Hearing an unhinged giggle from above, both boys looked up to see Brother Ecstatic creeping down the stairs.

"Oh, no. I lost my knife. Brother, could you lend me another one? *He-hehe-he!*" Ecstatic chuckled.

The basement door swung open. Berserk stepped out and swung an axe, decapitating the first person he saw. The kid dropped to the floor, and the screaming started. Ecstatic rushed down the stairs to block the front entrance, and kids started rushing to the back door. The sliding glass door was the only thing stopping kids from running directly into Sight, who waited patiently outside, looking in. Cornered in the kitchen, kids desperately backed up against the wall as Berserk hacked and slashed everyone in his path. The louder the kids screamed, the angrier his swings became. He could barely tolerate the noise; it fueled his pursuit of letting the anger get the better of him.

Sight raised a walkie-talkie. "Berserk, it's time to move on to the next part of the plan."

Berserk breathed deeply, holding his drenched weapon. His chest heaved as he swung his axe one last time into the corpse at his feet, chopping into their abdomen. He wiped blood from his mask and stared at the crying teenagers whose bodies hadn't yet met his axe. He looked back at his massacre with admiration and nodded to his brother.

"After this, we'll control this town," Sight said through a narrow space between the door and frame. "Make sure to call Noah with the new walkie from that generous officer."

Berserk walked past Ecstatic, exited the house, and climbed into a parked car. He fired it up and sped down the street toward his next act of destruction.

Sight opened the sliding glass door all the way and glanced at the surviving partygoers. As his eyes scanned the room, screams ascended with each passing second. He hadn't hurt anyone yet, but his presence was equally horrifying to all. He nodded and waved Ecstatic into the kitchen.

"Brother, please get these lovely people into the basement and tie them up. It's time to bait the people responsible for our brother's death."

CHAPTER 8

NO BACKUP

Noah stood in front of a board whose pushpins, notes, and images tied together the night's events thus far. Michaels approached him with more papers.

"Here's the rest of it, sir," Michaels informed him.

"Thanks," Noah said, "Is everyone here?"

"Yeah. Just waiting on your word to start."

Noah pinned the last documents to the board and waved the officers to gather around.

"Okay, this evening was a lot more than we bargained for. The good thing is, we have a lead on the suspects. Simon Kirk, the leader." Noah pointed to the white mask with black eyes. "Then we have the younger twin brothers, Austin and Gary." Noah pointed to the beast mask and the child mask, respectively.

"These are the brothers of Jay Kirk, sons of Jerrod Kirk, the guy who got busted almost ten years ago for drugs and guns," Michaels said. "Obviously, the kids fell from the same tree."

"As the guy who took out Jay," Noah began, "I have to insist we take extreme precautions with these three. This entire family is bad news. We're sending a team out tonight to hunt these guys down. Two shifts back-to-back until we get a lead on their location. Eyes open, boys. I'll announce the team shortly."

The crew broke off, and Michaels stood close to Noah.

"I say we stay here until we get something. I'd rather have our heads on straight until we have a lead," Michaels said. "Might be worth looking into the other missing people."

"Hey, Lieutenant. You're going to want to hear this," Officer Rusk hollered from a desk. "Got a call about a house party."

"Save it. We don't have the resources right now to waste on some teenagers," Noah explained.

"It's not just that. The call said something about a lot of screaming. They saw a masked man leave the scene," Officer Rusk added.

Noah exchanged a glance with Michaels.

"Change of plans," Noah said as he rushed to the door. "Michaels and I will check it out. Be ready for a call just in case we need backup."

As Noah and Michaels flew out of the precinct in their car, Brother Berserk radioed to Brother Sight. "They took the bait. Two officers are coming your way. I'll set the device now." Brother Berserk stepped out of his car and opened his trunk.

Noah and Michaels arrived at Devan's house to find the inside dark and quiet. They stepped out of the car, drawing their sidearms. Approaching the front of the house, they immediately noticed the front door was cracked open.

"I expect to walk into some sort of trap," Noah whispered. "Stay close, and keep your eyes peeled."

"Yes, sir," Michaels said.

Noah's radio spat out faint muttering.

"Didn't catch that," Noah responded. "Repeat. Over."

The response was slow to return.

"Come in. Don't have time for sloppy calls tonight," Noah barked, irritated. "Who's this? And what is it? Over."

"Good evening, Lieutenant," Berserk's voice came over the radio. "Hope you're enjoying the mess we're leaving for you to clean up."

"Well, that smart tone makes me think this is Austin Kirk. Yes, you did leave quite a mess for me. But I've dealt with worse. Over."

"That's Berserk to you, asshole," Brother Berserk corrected him.

"How did you get this radio? Over." Noah asked.

"A friendly gesture from Officer Melville. I pried it from his cold dead hand. And if you're wondering, he didn't die peacefully. In pieces, though, absolutely," Berserk said with a sinister chuckle.

Noah peered at Michaels, looking more worried than before.

"Admitting to murder. That'll go over well for you. Hope you and your brothers don't have a problem with needles. Lethal injection isn't too comfortable, I hear. Over."

"None of us are going to see the inside of a jail. We all know that very well, Lieutenant. Don't worry; more death will come before mine."

"I'll see about that tonight, Austin," Noah promised. "Everyone has eyes out for you. You better pray you're smarter than your brother Jay. Over."

"Listen, you motherfucker! I'll cut your face off myself if you keep running your mouth like that to me!"

"Fuck you. I'll see you later, Austin. Over and out." Noah clicked off his radio.

"You really think he got Melville?" Michaels asked.

"We won't know for sure until we get this place checked out. Shoot everyone at the station a message to be on high alert. Eyes up in here."

Noah pushed the door open to see the horror he had expected. Several dead bodies were scattered across the floor, and the walls proved just as gruesome, with copious blood spatter. Noah signaled Michaels to search the living room as he proceeded down the hall to the kitchen. The house was silent, but Noah knew something awaited his presence. He turned into the kitchen to see Michaels turning the corner.

"Clear," Michaels whispered. "Do we do the basement first or second floor?"

"Basement. I don't think these two are stupid enough to trap themselves up there."

Michaels pulled the basement door open, and Noah began descending the stairs slowly. Michaels followed. The unfinished basement was damp and just as dark. Noah flipped the switch right before hearing the cracked glass of a bulb crunch beneath his shoe. He clicked on his flashlight to see a group of kids, four in all, tied up in the corner of the room. Noah holstered his gun and rushed to the kids. Instantly recognizing one of the girls as Maggie, the daughter of a family friend, Noah untied her gag.

"Hey, what happened here?" Noah asked.

Maggie caught her breath and started to cry. She grew louder as her sobbing intensified. Noah held her shoulders for comfort, but it didn't seem to calm her hysteria in the least.

"Hey, I'm going to need you to quiet down," Noah said in a soothing tone. "Please, just take it easy."

Though slightly more composed now, she still struggled to find her words.

"Three men...killed everyone...tied us up. They're still here...hiding," Maggie blurted between short, panicked breaths.

"Do you have any idea where they are?" Noah asked.

"No. They were walking all over the house after they tied us up. We heard their footsteps go up and down the stairs a lot," Maggie said.

Noah turned to Michaels. "We need to check upstairs right away."

Footsteps echoed just as the words left Noah's lips. They came from the top of the stairs. Several more steps sounded from right above them, pacing. The basement door creaked, and Noah rotated swiftly to Michaels, drawing his gun from its holster.

One step sounded on the stairs.

Michaels took a step closer.

Noah walked behind Michaels.

A second step sounded on the stairs.

Michaels reached for his radio. "Requesting backup at our location."

There was no response.

Noah held his gun firmly as he waited for the third step.

"This is the police. I'm ordering you to freeze. Do not continue—" Michaels started.

Bang!

A single deafening shot echoed around the room, and Michaels dropped to the ground. Noah looked down at his partner to see blood pouring from the back of his head. Then he looked up to see the masked figures descend further. He raised his gun only for a well-aimed bullet to knock it from his grip. Blood squirted from his hand as the firearm flew across the room. Noah gripped his wounded appendage to try and control the blood flow.

"Lieutenant Noah. It's great to meet you in person finally," Sight said, reaching the bottom of the stairs.

Ecstatic reached the bottom right behind his older brother. He went to Michaels and picked up the slain cop's gun. Then he retrieved Noah's.

"You just killed a police officer," Noah said, squeezing his bleeding hand under his opposite underarm. "There's an entire station that will make you regret that."

"Yet I hear no sirens. Do you know why, Lieutenant?" Sight asked.

Sight pulled his cell phone out of his pocket and showed Noah a live video of the station in flames. The front entrance was riddled with burnt wreckage, dead police officers, and a giant hole exposing the interior of the building.

Noah shook his head in disbelief.

"I'm afraid this is the current situation you find yourself in," Sight said. "Besides the remaining town residents, you're alone, with no backup, with the three of us still active. Now, I'll give you a chance to turn in Sullivan. If you do, I'll spare you the trouble of hurting you further."

"I don't know where he ran off to," Noah said. "I haven't seen the coward since your video debut. But I wouldn't tell you even if I did know."

Sight turned to Ecstatic. They stared at one another briefly. Sight nodded, turned, and shot Maggie right between the eyes. Her dead body slumped forward, and blood dripped onto the floor. The kids tied to her screamed into their gags, crying hysterically. Noah turned back to see the girl he watched grow up over the years soak her own clothes in blood.

Brother Sight stepped closer to Noah. "Don't think I won't finish the rest of them off, Lieutenant," he said, clicking the gun's hammer back. "Tell me what I want to know, or another one dies."

"These kids have nothing to do with this. Let them go, and I'll take you to Sullivan. Please."

Noah could feel Sight's eyes probing his head, trying to gauge his thoughts. He glanced at Ecstatic, whose attention had drifted to another part of the room. He used this opportunity to lunge at Sight, grabbing his arm and throwing it in the air. The force of motion resulted in two unintentional rounds fired into the ceiling. Noah heard the kids scream as he and Sight fell to the ground.

No sooner did they hit the floor and start scuffing than the butt of Ecstatic's gun cracked against the side of Noah's temple. Upon seeing blood spray to the ground and drip from his weapon, he giggled.

Sight rolled out of the way and quickly stood up.

"Brother, hold him down," Sight instructed, taking one of the pistols from Ecstatic and strolling over to the remaining three kids.

Ecstatic placed his shoe on Noah's cheek and rolled, directing the cop's line of sight to the corner. A fitting punishment for his ill-advised attempt—forcing him to face the violence Sight intended to visit on the kids. The four shots were quick and painless for the victims. All four kids sat on the floor, bound, now bleeding from fresh openings in their heads. The drippings of warm crimson were the only sounds as Sight stood still, letting the silence of death fall upon Noah's guilt-ridden mind. Sight shoved his gun into his waistband and walked over to Noah, where he knelt in front of him.

"It would be easy to finish you here. But I want this to be difficult for you, just like you made it for my older brother. I'm going to find Sullivan and deal with him first. After that, we will see what else we can do to the remaining citizens of this town. Only when I'm sure there's no one left will I find wherever you've chosen to hide and kill you myself. Until then, I will revel in the enjoyment of watching you slowly fall apart," Sight said. "In case you were looking for clarity, here's a parting gift for when you wake up." Sight dropped something next to Noah.

Noah strained to make out what it was but couldn't.

Sight and Ecstatic went upstairs, and Noah's ears traced the sound of their departure. As he faded in and out of consciousness, he looked at the five dead people he'd failed to save. Cindy came into his mind like a speeding car.

I couldn't save her, either.

All he wanted was to wake up next to Cindy, let her know he'd changed his mind, that he'd devote every second to her from now on. They would settle down for a simpler life, something they could enjoy together without turmoil. But Cindy wasn't here. And he'd watched a fellow officer die in front of him. It felt worse than a nightmare.

This was Noah's personal bad dream.

CHAPTER 9

ANYONE

"I just want it to be about us. We will figure this whole thing out. You and I are what's most important. So let's enjoy our time together," Noah said.

Cindy's hazel eyes hypnotized Noah every time. He couldn't fight the urge to drown in her beauty.

"I love you, Noah. Thank you for understanding. I don't want your work to be your life. Nor do I want to be the reason you lose it."

"You're all the life I want and need. For now, let it be about us."

Noah reached for Cindy's hand only to feel emptiness. Their eyes locked as she faded into the void she already knew as her home. Noah felt reality setting in.

"It's all a bad dream."

Noah slowly emerged from his unconsciousness. Blood from his head made his rise even more challenging, peeling the red slime like a wet Band-Aid. He felt something foreign in his hand. As the items attempted to slip from his fingers, he gripped them and raised them into view.

They were Polaroids—pictures of the missing people, all confirmed dead. A shot of Benny Kalfa just as Noah had found him. Mark Kens with his mangled jaw on the floor of some vacant building. Lynn Perry's eyes gouged out, drenched in blood and other fluids from her pierced sockets. Jess Summerson with a heavy-duty zip tie pinching the skin around her neck, leaving her face a ghostly gray with bulging veins. The last, Mary Weiss, a knife still stuck in her chest, with several other visible stab wounds.

Partially out of disbelief and lack of strength, Noah dropped the polaroids to the ground. That was when he noticed the words on the back of each. With careful positioning, he deciphered the message behind the pictures: *Long Live The Kirk Name!*

His body, mainly his head, still struggled to cooperate with him. He climbed to his feet, careful not to step on his deceased partner. He climbed the stairs, still dizzy from the direct hit to his temple. He gripped the railing and slowly pulled himself up. He went to the kitchen and wiped the blood from his head with a hand towel from the counter. He dug through the medicine cabinet in the bathroom and covered his head wounds with small bandages. He opened the coat closet, pulled out a scarf, and tightly wrapped his hand to control the bleeding. He looked at his phone to check its battery life. He tried calling the station, hoping someone might answer. After a few failed attempts, he knew the worst was true.

Noah exited the house to see his patrol car on fire. Since the whole thing was engulfed, he assumed it had been set as soon as the Kirks left. Without options, he made his way to the station, hoping to find someone alive. Failing that, he could make use of what was left of the building. From what he saw in the video, the interior was still intact. Maybe that was his mind telling him there was still hope.

The streets were empty as Noah approached the wreckage of his safe place. He wondered if he could get backup from neighboring towns or if they'd already been alerted by such an explosion. Headlights distracted him from his current thoughts. A fleet of cars came toward him, their lights flashing in his direction. He waved one down to see Bob O'Connor in front of the fleet.

"Bob, what's this? Where are you all going?" Noah asked.

"We have families, Noah," Bob explained. "We need to think about them. Between our summer homes and other relatives, we think it's best to protect the people of this town elsewhere. For now, at least."

"I don't blame you at all," Noah admitted. "Do you know if anyone else stayed back? I don't know what I can do against these guys on my own."

"No one told me. I gathered these people, and they all followed my lead. Listen, reach out when you know it's safe. Be careful. I wish I could do more," Bob said, slowly riding off.

Noah watched the fleet pass him. He waved at some of the people he recognized and stood still until the last car faded into the darkness. He turned back and headed into the station. The smoke was dimly lit by the streetlights. He saw the entrance and the scattered bodies in the entranceway. The remaining squad cars were either on fire or burned so thoroughly that they were nearly unrecognizable. Noah walked in and looked around at the interior. Desks and papers were thrown in every direction. Several dead officers blocked the way to his office. He clicked on the first radio he found.

"This is Lieutenant Noah," he announced. "Does anyone read me? Are there any officers currently available for assistance?"

Silence filled the room save for a persistent radio static that echoed in his throbbing head.

"Can anyone read me?"

This was the closest Noah had come to giving up since the entire collapse of the town started. Most residents were dead or fleeing, and the officers who swore to protect and serve were gone too. He'd had high hopes for Michaels turning his behavior around. One of his first decisions as Lieutenant would've been to promote Michaels. All his choices slowly unraveled, as his options were scarce with no support available.

"Over. Come in, Noah."

The radio response was a relief to Noah's ringing ears. He gripped the radio with desperation.

"Who's this?" Noah asked. "Magnusson?"

"Yes, sir. I was out on patrol after leaving the hospital when the explosion happened. I passed by discreetly but saw one of the brothers, so I tucked my squad car away. I'm hiding out in a parked car. They found my squad car and torched it immediately."

"Where are you now?" Noah asked.

"I'm down the block from Mac's Bar," Magnusson answered.

The answer clicked in Noah's mind. Mac's Bar was one of the rowdiest bars in town. Mostly known for the Adam Crew, run by Adam Pannella. With a reputation for beating up anyone who mouthed off to him and spending more nights in jail than anyone else in town, he was known as the guy to leave alone. His crew, fellow lowlifes who drank too much and provoked people into fights, hardly ever left his side. Not unless it was to bang women from the bar or take a piss in the back alley.

"Is the Adam crew still there?"

"I think so. I heard a lot of commotion in there."

"I want you to confirm it for me," Noah instructed. "I want a list of everyone in there and report back. I'll be there in thirty minutes. I'll explain everything when I arrive. In the meantime, be safe."

Noah clicked the radio off and went to his office. He looked in his top drawer and grabbed his sidearm, shoving it down into his waistband. After snapping a few photos of the evidence board to send to Magnusson, he walked to the gun room but stopped when he heard shuffling in the kitchen. He drew the sidearm, walking slowly toward the sound. The shuffling grew louder as he approached. Noah turned the corner quickly to find Sullivan trying to hide behind the cabinet to the left of the door.

"Jesus Christ, Sullivan," Noah said. "Have you been hiding here this whole time? I almost shot you."

"Did anyone survive?" Sullivan asked.

"Just Magnusson. Everyone else is gone. What the hell are you doing?"

"Noah, I'm so ready for retirement. I spent my entire career barely doing more than settling screaming matches in peoples' yards. Jay Kirk was the first pursuit I'd ever had. Now his family is killing people in our quiet town. I don't have the guts to settle this. I can't handle those creeps."

Noah's head dropped in disappointment and anger. If he'd had any respect for Sullivan before he arrived, it was now officially gone.

"So, you're going to cower here until Magnusson dies or I die? What's your plan? Because those three assholes are still out there, and they're looking for you! They want the two of us to come forward."

"Yes, that's right. What are you doing about them?"

Noah rushed at Sullivan and pulled him by the shirt, slamming him against the wall. He pinned his arm across Sullivan's neck to brace him from evading.

"Get...your hands...off…of me!" Sullivan scolded, struggling against Noah's hold.

"You cowardly piece of shit. You were out there when all those people died. Now you're going to hide here and wait for them to quietly leave when they're done? They aren't leaving until this town rots away to nothing!" Noah shouted. He released his grip on Sullivan and made for the door. "I'm going to stop them if it's my last night alive. Good luck here by yourself, asshole."

Even if they crossed paths in the future, Noah would only see an empty man and never a former mentor. Noah left the station with the intention of never seeing Sullivan alive again.

CHAPTER 10

RALLY THE TROOPS

Magnusson stayed low in his car when he returned to it. He routinely walked out, stepped in to spy the patrons of Mac's Bar, then sneaked back to slump down in the driver's seat every ten minutes. He was sure the Adam Crew locked eyes with him a few times, but they hardly budged from their usual antics inside the bar. Adam Pannella was the calmest when drinking but the most violent when fights broke out. Magnusson even theorized that alcohol made Adam's blood craving more intense. He hoped he wouldn't see that anger, given how the night was already going.

A faint tap on the window from Noah made Magnusson jump and grip his gun. Noah pulled the door open and hopped in.

"So, what do we have?" he asked.

Magnusson looked at Noah's bandage, surprised he was still walking around. "What the hell happened to you?"

"I met Simon and Gary, but they let me live. Michaels wasn't so lucky. What happened to Melville?"

Magnusson shook his head. "Ran off to be a hero. Haven't heard from him since."

"I got a call from Austin before I went into the house. I think Melville had the same rotten luck as Michaels. We'll get them. Any progress with Adam's crew?"

"The crew is all there. Four, including Adam. When I checked ten minutes ago, one cook, one bartender, and one other patron. What are you going to do, sick the Adam Crew on these psychos?"

Magnusson started to chuckle and looked at Noah's blank stare, realizing they had the same idea without the sarcasm in between. Panic immediately set into Magnusson's chest.

"That's exactly what I'm going to do. But with me leading the way, we have a real chance at getting these guys," Noah said.

"Have you completely lost it? I mean, I see you took a hit to the head, and we're horribly out of options at this point, but this is just the lowest we can go," Magnusson complained.

Noah also knew his plan was as risky as it sounded. Adam and his crew were no safer than the Kirk brothers by a long shot. Part of him had already heard the inevitable *Go fuck yourself* and wanted to back out and start fresh with a new idea. But the Kirk Brothers were still out there; their body count already piled high.

Noah opened his car door and stepped out.

"We are out of options. I'm going."

"Hey, wait a minute. Are you sure you want to do this?" Magnusson asked.

"Look, these guys have killed close to forty people already, and we still have a few hours until sunrise.

They're not going to surrender, and they sure as hell aren't going peacefully in handcuffs. Honestly, I don't want to take them peacefully after seeing what I've seen tonight. I'm going to make sure those three are the last to die. Stay here if you want. I'm not waiting any longer." Noah exited, slamming the car door.

"Goddamnit." Magnusson opened his car door.

Noah stepped into the bar with Magnusson right behind him.

Everyone inside the bar could feel the tense moment. The bartender looked up briefly and then headed to Adam's section.

Adam glanced at the newcomer and stared over his shoulder before returning to his beer. His vocal henchman, Jordan Baron, however, reacted differently.

"So, two pigs walk into a bar..." Jordan said before chuckling and choking on his beer.

"Good evening, gentlemen," Magnusson said. "I see you're on your routine night in town."

"Suck my dick, Magnusson. I didn't forget about you pinning that car break-in on my little brother," Peter Hutch said, standing and slamming his beer on the bar.

"Take it easy, Hutch. We're just here to talk to you all." Noah stepped forward slowly.

The group reacted by standing. All except for Adam, who continued to sip his drink calmly.

"Looks like Petey wants a little more than a chat, Detective." Ryan Marc, the quiet one in the group, seemed excited to watch a potential brawl. As the frequent lookout, he was often left out of the excitement.

90

His posture shifted, waiting for something exciting to happen.

"Let's just take it easy. Can everyone do that?" Noah stepped closer to Adam, hoping to get his attention. "Now, I'm sure some of you heard the commotion from around town. Many people have already lost their lives, and, as embarrassing as it is, I've run out of sane options. I don't have a good relationship with any of you—"

"I'll fucking say. A brotha like yourself ain't have no place with the badge on. Police ain't for us." Jordan gestured back and forth to himself and Noah, indicating their skin color before returning his attention to the TV above the bar. Noah ignored the remark.

"Quiet, Baron," Magnusson said.

"Why don't you shut the fuck up, Magnusson? Maybe show some respect to your fucking superior." Peter's hand trembled with rage, clutching his beer firmly.

Magnusson smirked, getting closer to Peter. "So should you, prick."

It only took a few seconds for Peter to clear the distance to grab Magnusson by the collar and slam him against the wall.

Noah pulled his sidearm, pointing it at Peter.

"Hutch, it would be smart of you to put him down. If you want to take your anger out on someone, tonight is the night I'll allow that to happen."

"What the fuck are you going on about, Noah?" Jordan asked. "You got one of those cop fetishes?"

"Fuck you, Baron. I'm talking about the Kirk brothers. Jay Kirk's younger siblings. They're ripping this town apart, and I need your help to stop them. I'm out of ideas. We can kill each other here, or you can help me and get some more freedom from what's left of the police force. What's it gonna be?"

"Give me your gun," Adam said, setting his drink down and walking to Noah. "We carry, or you can die on the street alone."

"Don't do it, Noah," Magnusson said.

"Shut up, you piece of shit," Peter yelled into Magnusson's face. He looked at Adam, fuming with rage. "Let's just do it here. If they're the last of the town's pigs, we can get this done, and no one will bother us again."

Adam ran out of patience with Peter's behavior. "I'll kill you right in front of these fucking pigs if you don't let him go right now. Stop fucking around."

Peter shoved Magnusson into the wall once more and let him go. He returned to his spot near the bar.

Noah didn't have any clue as to why someone so big took orders from Adam. There was a lot of history between the two, so if Peter was this obedient, it was likely for a good reason. And Noah didn't need to know that reason at the moment.

"Give me your gun or no deal. I'll kill these fuckers myself and be back here before the last call." Adam extended his hand, hoping Noah would comply.

Magnusson gripped Noah's shoulder. "There's gotta be a way other than enlisting criminals into our ranks."

Noah handed Adam the gun. He'd faced more fear in the basement hours ago than he did now, surrendering to local felons. He was confident Adam craved control over rebellion.

"I'll follow your lead, but I don't follow your rules if we're hunting. Got it?" Adam pointed to his crew. "They all get guns, too."

"We'll stop at the police station and see what's left. Come on." Noah gestured for everyone to follow.

"Wait," Magnusson said, "no plan? No organization? Noah, tell me we aren't running out there with only a few more guns blazing. We need to be smart about this."

Noah gripped Magnusson's shoulder. "Adam has been hunting all his life. He's a tracker. Baron is useless, but the other two have tracking skills and can get us to the Kirks before they find us. That's why I'm asking them for assistance. I could care less about their previous crap."

"I better get full auto for that remark," Jordan chided. "Asshole."

They made their way back to the police station, hoping what remained was enough to keep them alive for a few more hours.

CHAPTER 11

BIG GAME HUNTING

Noah searched every desk at the station. He found a few .38s that some officers had stashed in their desks and ammo to go with them.

Magnusson found two shotguns with the help of their small militia.

Peter entered from the kitchen, carrying several bags of chips. "Since no one would notice anyway, the vending machine is open for business in case anyone's hungry."

"Always thinking about your stomach, fat ass," Jordan chuckled.

Peter immediately retorted with the middle finger.

Adam exited the locker room sporting a bullet-proof vest. "Always wanted to wear one of these. Found a few more." He tossed three onto the desk in front of him.

"What's the plan, Noah?" Magnusson asked.

Adam's crew strapped themselves with the vests and slid the .38s into their waistbands. Peter grabbed a shotgun and began feeding shells into it.

Noah didn't have a thought-out plan yet. He contemplated how much he wanted to involve Adam's crew to take down these psychopaths. There wasn't much he could keep from them without sabotaging their aid in saving the town.

"The only confirmed place we know of their whereabouts is the abandoned lot. They had their car parked where Benny Kalfa disappeared. We start there. Is there anything of significance beyond those trees?"

Noah looked around at the blank stares. It was already going south, even with four more heads.

"There used to be an old shack out there," Adam said. "We used it to smoke in as teenagers, but I know a few hunters who use it during cold mornings. It's pretty obvious if you know it's there. I don't think these prissy townsfolk knew about it."

"That's only a mile or two from the abandoned steel mill," Magnusson said. "Melville was headed there before he went quiet. We could be walking into a trap. If these guys are that smart, something is likely waiting for us there."

The warning didn't seem to faze anyone. They all made their way to the entrance.

"We have the numbers and firepower. I wouldn't be worried if I were you," Peter said, lightly brushing Magnusson's shoulder as he pushed past.

"We start at the shack. Fewer places to hide. We can surround them if they're held up there. Does that work for everyone?" Noah asked.

The group nodded.

They walked quietly with the understanding that a car would attract attention and conversation would give away the size of the group. They spread out further as they went. Ryan signaled to them frequently, making use of his lookout skills. Adam and Noah walked together at the back of the group.

"It may not mean anything to you," Noah said, "but I appreciate you giving up your evening for this."

Adam chuckled. "What can I say? Despite you selling out and going in the wrong direction, you were my oldest friend out of middle school."

"If you hate this town so much, why have you stayed here so long?" Noah asked.

Adam wasn't proud of being the town's tough guy. He'd gotten tied up in crime shortly after graduating high school, and nothing ever panned out in terms of legit work. Those who knew his equally troublesome father were the only ones willing to hire him for odd jobs. It was comfortable for him to have steady work and not try to rebuild his life elsewhere, so he stuck to his occasional freelance opportunities and worked with other convicted felons.

"Once you get past people who look at you like you're shit, and you return that look, it's all the same wherever I go. So why not stay in Hyde cove, a place I already know? Besides, us small-town folk aren't supposed to leave."

"That's bullshit, and you know it," Noah remarked.

"Cindy knew it just as I did," Adam said, feeling the tension between him and Noah. "That's why she left. She knew you were never getting out of here as long as you felt the need to serve the town." He stopped when Noah blocked his way.

"I devoted everything to this job so I could give us both better lives one day. I had the chance to go elsewhere, but I wanted to keep my home and the people I've known my whole life safe. It's sad you don't see that. And it haunts me that Cindy never got to see it, either." Noah walked on without waiting for Adam to catch up.

Ryan raised his fist in the air, signaling everyone to freeze.

Noah seldom got scared, but he shivered when he saw the signal. He wasn't ready to move forward and see more people he'd grown up with end up dead. More bodies were piled in his typically peaceful, compliant town than he ever felt possible. His hand went to his holster, gripping the handle of his gun firmly.

Adam snapped his fingers twice.

Peter and Jordan huddled by Noah.

Magnusson approached Ryan slowly.

"Okay, boys. We have three targets. Peter, head to the right side for a vantage point. Jordan, get into the shack quietly, and we'll be right behind you."

"What about Ryan and Magnusson?" Noah asked.

A high-caliber gunshot echoed in the trees, and Ryan's limp body collapsed to the ground.

Magnusson ducked nearby, out of the line of fire.

"Motherfucker," Adam growled. "I'll kill all three myself!" He ducked from tree to tree, quickly approaching his fallen friend.

Noah slowed his pace and signaled the other two to follow. "Adam! Adam, wait up!"

More shots came. The muzzle flashes were sporadic. Bark ripped from trees, and dirt flew into the air. Adam dodged them carefully, using trees as shields and shadows as cover. He tucked himself against the shack's front door, away from their attackers' line of sight. He looked across at Ryan, whose head now tipped like a splattered cherry pie. He slowly rose and peeked through the window, seeing shadows move from inside the wooden hideout.

Up ahead, Adam put two fingers in the air, followed by one that pointed to the shack.

"Two armed men inside," Noah told the others. "Peter, get to the side so we can try to hit them from another angle. I have to get to Magnusson. Jordan, try and get to Adam if you can."

Both men nodded and went to their destinations.

Noah offered cover fire as he crossed the larger opening where trees weren't as dense. His only reference of distance to the shooters was the muzzle flashes from inside the shack. Jordan moved faster than Peter, whose bulk exceeded the tree cover. Jordan made it to Adam in several quick dashes.

Noah saw the second muzzle flash move toward Peter, so he emptied his gun at that window. The second shooter stopped, and Peter ducked down in the distance. He was hidden even from Noah, so he knew he'd figure out his next move while out of visibility.

Magnusson stuck his head out hesitantly, making himself known to Noah. "Hey, you hurt?"

"I'm good. Didn't want to lose my head, too. I think the third brother is out here somewhere. Saw some movement in the woods, but I wasn't sure."

Noah looked up, seeing moonlight cut through the darkness to blanket the wooded landscape. "Head in there to give Adam and Jordan backup. I'll keep an eye out for the third. Last thing we need is to get picked off or pinned down by a sharpshooter."

Magnusson ducked down and rushed toward the cabin.

"We barge in on three." Adam slowly counted and then turned the door handle.

Jordan checked his ammo, ready to avenge Ryan's death.

The door swung open, and Jordan rushed in firing. Adam followed close behind. Shattering glass and creaking wood echoed all around them. They were quick to duck when their targets answered with shots of their own.

Gary couldn't control his laughter. "We're killing this entire town tonight, Berserk, aren't we?"

"You pricks are fucking dead!" Austin cocked his gun, waiting for Adam and Jordan's next move.

The room went silent and still.

Adam listened closely for sound and movement from the brothers. Anything to get an advantage.

"Maybe we killed them!" Gary shrieked with excitement.

The window exploded, showering him with glass. Peter continued to fire from the side of the cabin.

Austin crawled to the corner of the room, sheltering behind a cabinet. His walkie-talkie clicked on.

"Looks like you could use some help," Simon said. From his position in the woods, he peered down the scope of his rifle, locking on the cabin. The place had become a warzone. "How many people are trying to kill you?"

"At least three. Fucking shoot them already!" Austin leaned out from his cover, firing blindly. None of his shots landed.

Adam stood to get Peter's attention. "Hey, how many do you see?"

"Two on the other side of that wall. I'm going to get closer to—"

Bang!

A distant shot rang through the trees again. Adam's eyes followed as Peter's limp corpse slammed into the tree behind him and hit the ground. Brain matter, strips of flesh, and bone fragments clung to the tree. "Fucking third one keeps picking us off."

"And he'll kill the rest of you too!" Austin approached swiftly, aiming at Adam.

Jordan reached up, firing at Austin. The bullets tore through his hand, severing two fingers. His gun fell to the ground, and Jordan let out a victorious chuckle.

"Got one!" Jordan laughed.

Austin crawled back to his hiding place, squeezing his hand tight. He groaned, letting his agony known to everyone still inside.

Gary went to him.

"Do you need a Band-Aid, brother?" Gary asked.

"Just keep firing at them, you piece of shit!" Austin pressed his hand against his chest. The blood soaked into his clothing. He'd lost his power quicker than expected, but his rage continued to grow. Austin considered his brother's unpredictable mental state and inappropriate giggling outbursts. He wasn't confident in his ability to get this done.

Adam looked around the corner to see Gary reloading his gun sloppily. He aimed and fired. His shot resulted in a grunt and a thud.

Gary's body went slack in front of Austin.

"How's that for killing everyone, you fucking psycho?" Adam shouted. He checked his gun to see three shots remaining. He leaned over and whispered to Jordan: "How many shots do you have left?"

"Just one. I'm going to rush him, but I'll make it count." Jordan crouched, preparing to run.

"Wait. Jordan, wait—"

Jordan launched from behind the wall and dashed for Austin, gun pointed ahead of him. He neared Austin's position to see him pointing a sawed-off shotgun above his head. Though Jordan couldn't see the man's face, he felt certain he was smiling behind that mask.

Boom!

Adam didn't witness the violence, but when the blood showered over him, he knew it was over. Pieces flew around the room, even as high as the ceiling. The moist splat of what remained of Jordan's body made the playing field even for both sides. Despite his mangled hand, Austin chuckled at his victim, who now lay scattered in pieces.

"Even with three fingers, my shot is still spot on," Austin boasted. "Hey, do you want to come and see what remains of your friend? By my count, that's all that's left besides that fucking pig."

Adam stood, trying to get a view of his last target. His head peaked out to see the barrel pointing up at him. He just missed the blast as he fell back behind his cover. It had been a long time since Adam felt fear, especially in the town where he was the one to be feared.

His last three shots had to be used well. After all, he didn't know how many shells Austin had left.

Noah approached each tree with patience and care, employing silence and stealth. He figured he'd hear movement in advance of any attempt on his life, so he kept his faith in that logic. He had walked for quite a while and still hadn't come across anything. Then, finally, he spied a dark spot in the trees up ahead, where thick branches obscured the moon. Had he been one of these deranged people, he would've chosen it as a perfect spot for a vantage point. He only took a few more steps before he saw the rifle.

He drew his pistol, trying not to let the holster make the slightest sound. He kept to the shadows, drawing closer to the gunman. He suspected it was the leader of the three maniacs.

Simon kept his eye to the scope, watching the mess unfold within the cabin. He had added two victims of his own to the body count. Now he waited for one of the brothers to exit and give him the signal to move forward with their plan. A pistol clicked by his ear. When he tried to reach for his sidearm, he felt Noah's gun touch the temple of his mask.

"Here's how we're going to play this. Whatever fucked-up plan you have next, it's over. Put the rifle on the ground, or I put the side of this mask through your skull. Slowly."

Simon cooperated without saying a word. The rifle fell into the grass, and he raised his hands above his head.

Noah dug the pistol into his back.

"Move."

They walked slowly down the hill toward the shootout.

Austin stood with some effort, using the sawed-off to prop himself up. "Two shots left—one for your face and one for the pig out there. Now, I don't expect to find that colored fella in the dark so easily, but maybe I'll wait until morning and deal with him properly."

Adam's fear eased a bit. Now he knew the ammo count for everyone in the room. He had to be smart. Those shells couldn't be wasted with sloppy shots.

"Colored fella?" Adam asked from behind the wall. "I didn't realize you were a racist from the 1960s. But I get why you're afraid. I took your brother out."

Austin's deep laughter went on, leading Adam to understand he wasn't afraid. "The retard didn't stand a chance. Come out, let's do this like men."

"How do I know you won't be a fucking snake and pull something fast?" Adam asked.

No response followed. A mild thud echoed across the cabin. Adam looked over the wall to see Austin's mask. It rested on the floor, dirt and blood stains adding to the haunting disguise.

"Look in my eye when I kill you, trailer trash."

Adam walked over, standing tall in front of Austin. He gazed into his dark, hollow brown eyes, seeing a much smaller man. The tension of controlling his anger from fully releasing showed on his pale face. Adam thought the mask had made the man bigger, more fearsome. Behind it was nothing but another lowlife he wanted to beat until his knuckles were raw and bloody. They stared one another down, each waiting for the other to make a move.

"On three?"

"On three."

The sawed-off cocked.

The hammer on the pistol clicked back.

"One—"

The shots from outside tore into Austin's arm before he could get any further. He swung, trying to aim at Magnusson, who approached quickly. Adam returned to his cover, letting the cop take over for him. He'd lost all of his friends in less than two hours, so allowing a cop to die or win the evening was preferable to perishing at the hands of a lunatic himself.

Austin dropped his shotgun and kneeled in front of the window. Magnusson rushed the empty frame, quickly climbing in to continue his assault on Austin.

Now soaked in his own blood, Austin surrendered without speaking a word. He glared at Magnusson, who stood above him with a partially loaded gun. Probably half a clip.

"Good work, Pannella," Magnusson addressed Adam. "Shame the rest of you didn't make it."

"Yeah, I bet you're heartbroken over it." Adam grabbed Austin's shotgun and clicked the chamber open. One shot left. He would've been in two pieces from that distance. He passed the weapon to Magnusson. "Thanks. Glad I'm still here."

Noah whistled from outside.

Adam and Magnusson looked out, seeing Noah descending the hill with Simon, the latter towering over the former.

"Looks like your evening is over. Get up." Magnusson ordered Austin, pulling him outside.

Adam followed.

Noah stopped when he saw Magnusson and Adam exit with Austin. His hands hung limply at his sides, both dripping blood. He was clearly out of the fight.

"Only you two made it out?" Noah asked.

"Just us," Magnusson said. "We got one of them, though."

Simon stepped forward, forcing Noah to grip his arm and yank him back. "Brother, how are you? Are you dying?"

"Doing better than the other three we left on the ground."

Magnusson cracked Austin in the face, opening a gash just below his eye.

"That'll be the last time you touch me, fucking pig." Austin spat at Magnusson. He clenched tightly as the pain radiated throughout his mangled arms.

Magnusson wanted to retort aggressively, but he felt it was a waste. The battle was over, and only one brother had a promising chance of surviving the night.

"What's the move, Noah? Finishing it all right here and now?" Adam asked.

"This only stops when we're done with our plan."

Noah pressed his pistol into Simon's ribs. "Shut up." He then faced Magnusson. "We'll take them back to the station. We can get in touch with other units from surrounding towns. They'll sit tight in a cell for now."

"We aren't done. We have more left for you and your shitty town," Austin said. "How many more people do you think can escape before a bomb or two goes off?"

"Shut your fucking mouth!" Adam swung his pistol into Austin's face.

His head dropped, releasing blood from his swollen lips. Faint laughter emerged from the defeated maniac.

"What could you possibly find funny?" Noah asked.

Austin didn't stop. The group looked at him as his laughter echoed through the woods. Magnusson's expression showed worry. Noah didn't know how to get him to snap out of it, and Adam's patience had run thin.

"Enough of this," Adam said.

The shot blew through Austin's head, splattering Magnusson in hot brains. The limp corpse collapsed and bled out on the ground. With this death, the body count had reached a height not even Noah could see over, not after the night's horrors.

"I'll finish this, Brother Berserk." Simon dropped his head, finally facing sorrow for the evening.

"It *is* finished, Kirk." Noah kicked out Simon's leg, dropping him to his knees.

A whistle pierced through the trees. All three pistols aimed in its direction only to see Sullivan walking toward them with his tiny .38 firmly gripped in hand.

"It's me," he said. "Glad to see you got this little mess taken care of."

"Glad to see you've finished hiding. Retirement sounds better than helping your town these days, huh?" Magnusson asked.

"Shut up, Magnusson." Sullivan eyed Adam, looking him up and down.

Despite all he'd done to help the police force this evening, Adam could feel Sullivan's hateful eyes on him.

"Adam Pannella," Sullivan said. "I'm surprised you left the bar to help out."

"King Pig Sullivan. I hope the couch supports you better than your desk did."

Sullivan hadn't been disrespected like that since his run-in with Jay Kirk. He faced Adam, standing taller than him, not to mention significantly heavier with his bulging belly.

"Enough out of both of you. We get this guy back to holding and end this shit tonight."

Bang!

Noah didn't think there was anything left for them tonight. The death toll had surpassed what he imagined it could reach, and now the man who'd been his boss and mentor for nearly a decade was gone.

Sullivan's head barely hung onto his neck. The mass of what remained had been burned from the high-caliber shot.

Magnusson fled behind a tree.

Adam followed close behind.

"It's almost done, Noah. I can feel it." Simon swung his head into Noah's groin and broke from his grasp. He took off into the dark woods toward the anonymous shooter.

"Magnusson, with me. This ends tonight."

Adam gripped Noah's sleeve. "What about me? Where am I going?"

"Home. I don't need a higher body count than I already have. Lock your doors and keep away until you hear from me."

"Not much of the hiding type, Noah."

"I know, but you're not dying because of me. Thanks for everything." Noah pulled from Adam's grip.

Noah and Magnusson rushed into the darkness, unaware of who remained to aid the massacre that had forever changed Hyde Cove.

CHAPTER 12

FAMILY UNITED

Magnusson's breathing proved a distraction, and Noah wondered if it drew more attention to them. How Magnusson could still be this alarmingly out of breath after the night they'd had boggled Noah. Keeping yourself in shape was a habit that seldom occurred within the Hyde Cove Police Department. Not Noah, though. Health was the only other thing on his mind when he wasn't working.

Noah stopped, taking cover behind a tree.

Magnusson's eyes lit up like they'd glimpsed salvation.

"Breathe, man. How did you let yourself get this bad?" Noah asked.

Magnusson couldn't reply. With his struggling lungs, he felt like he was drawing breath through a pinched straw. He threw up a finger, telling Noah to wait.

Noah grew impatient. Every second they stood still was a second the oldest brother got farther away. Worse yet, he could soon be off doing something to further unravel their already devastated town.

"Listen, I'm going ahead. Collect yourself and catch up with me." Noah checked his ammo. Fully loaded. "I have enough to cover myself, but if they're stocked with automatics, I'll need backup sooner than later."

"I'm thirty seconds behind you," Magnusson promised.

Noah paced himself, walking and then pausing to listen for snapping branches or footsteps. Brother Sight couldn't have gotten much further than him.

Who was the mysterious shooter? Who besides the three brothers could possibly be behind the night's horrors? What had Noah missed? His thoughts kept his mind occupied. He lost focus. Each step brought him deeper into the black woods and further from his goal.

Footsteps sounded rapidly from behind, pulling Noah from his thoughts. He whirled around to lay eyes on Magnusson. His fellow officer stopped in front of him, holding his substantial gut, still breathing heavily.

"If you needed more time, you could've—" Magnusson dropped to a crouch.

Magnusson wasn't out of breath, not any more than usual. Instead, his hand attempted to contain the blood flow from a serious abdominal wound. But his fingers barely held anything in. Within seconds of his arrival, he hit the ground face-first.

"Hey, Magnusson. Get up. Come on." Noah tugged at his unconscious friend, but his eyes remained shut. There was no hope of ever waking him.

A gun clicked by Noah's ear. "Look straight ahead."

Noah released Magnusson and stood up, letting his gun fall to the ground.

"One last play in the cards, Noah. Then it's all over," Simon said.

Branches snapped behind them. Noah turned his head to see a silhouette standing nearby. The person stepped from the shadows to reveal a familiar face. A tattered face from the past.

But it can't be, not after all this time.

Simon's gun cracked the back of Noah's head, causing the faint memory of an old enemy to tumble into blackness.

Noah could smell the meal on the table. Cindy waited patiently for her food.

"I don't mind. You can start without me," she said.

Noah loved when she ran her hair to one side of her head, and she'd done it frequently this evening.

Date nights were rare with his long hours. After constant arguing, Noah managed to find a small restaurant that would take a last-minute reservation. After quickly finding appropriate attire, a small dinner date was shaping up to be a successful recharge for a struggling relationship.

"I'm so excited for us to spend more time together this weekend. I don't know what they have you doing at the station, but it's too much if you ask me."

"Actually, I'm there all weekend. I didn't tell you?" Noah asked.

"That's okay. I really hope this job doesn't get you killed one day."

Noah smiled, assuring her of his confidence. "I couldn't imagine even coming close."

Noah's eyes opened. A bad dream, perhaps, or a vision that never happened. He couldn't be sure anymore, not after yet another severe head injury. Objects in the room danced around as he tried to focus through his abrupt awakening. Bright bulbs lit the vacant steel mill where he sat bound to a chair. He recognized the squad car parked inside from the remaining red light flashing back and forth. Melville's dead body, gashed at the throat, rested on the car's hood.

He could taste blood. He could smell it, too, like a strong cologne he'd over-sprayed for a first date trying to make a good impression. He heard the door open, but his faded vision didn't inform him who had entered.

"I think you hit him a tad too hard," the mysterious figure said.

"Not the first time tonight. Still, he'll understand." Simon's mask unclipped and fell to the ground. He slapped Noah's face, bringing him back to his destroyed reality. "Time to wake up."

Noah stared into the empty eyes before looking up at the unmasked man. He appeared remarkably well-kempt for a man whose face had hid behind a mask all night.

He had messy beard stubble and greasy black hair hanging below his shoulders. His glaring brown eyes housed a look of impending doom. The wisest of the three and certainly the most put-together.

112

"W-where…am I?" Noah stammered. His words felt heavy in his mouth. All he could do now was take his time and hope it wasn't abruptly cut short.

"If I were you, I'd be more concerned about who I really am," said someone unseen in the background.

Simon stepped aside as another masked man entered the room. His mask, pure black, had no facial features. Neither mouth nor nose. Not even eyes. A man was inside the mask, but Noah's injured state made him believe otherwise.

The man kneeled in front of Noah, his black mask proving just as featureless up close.

"Have masked men haunted you this evening, Lieutenant Noah?"

The voice turned Noah's stomach. The familiarity within the confusion reached frightening levels. Yet he couldn't grasp the identity. "More so the good people of this town," Noah said, "but I'd be lying if I said I won't step in a Halloween store again."

"These masks are not for frightening children or winning costume contests; they're meant to be a memory burned into the brains of everyone who witnessed them tonight. Whatever happens to us, these faces are what you'll see when you look back on the history of Hyde Cove. After all, no one ever gave our real faces any value. We were doomed to be monsters forever."

Noah was coming back to reality, feeling more like himself again. "I don't recall seeing you on those TVs at the fair or at the party house. Seems to me like you're taking credit for other peoples' work."

"Well, that could be an assumption of yours. You'll probably recognize this face instead."

The black mask slid from his head, revealing the face of haunting memories—Jay Kirk. His cheek bore a bad scar that stretched from his jawline to the base of his nose. Another small scar dotted the flesh just below his bottom lip where the bullet exited that night. This old wound no doubt accounted for the slight lisp Noah had detected.

"How?" Noah asked.

"I survived. A mangled face wasn't enough to stop me from running. I collected myself and kept going. Sure, it was hard. A record of repeated arrests and a deterring face is enough to stop just about anyone from hiring me. So, I thought it best to return to where it all started."

"My aunt kept my trips to town private, and I got to spend time with my three younger brothers. Then it occurred to me that no one in Hyde Cove would treat them well with my father in prison and their oldest brother gunned down by the town's noblest officer. I planned. I taught them. And I gave them the proper guidance to make the Kirk name stick in Hyde Cove forever. Do you know what tonight is, Noah?"

Noah shook his head, but he knew the answer.

"Eight years since my father was sentenced to life in prison. Eight agonizing years since the family started to crumble."

"Those were his choices," Noah said. "And you made your own choices after that. Both of you let bad decisions ruin your family."

"People talked long before his sentencing. My name was ruined before he broke the law a second time."

"That may be true, but I'm not responsible for ruining your name. I only stopped you from making your father's mistakes. But you're so far past what he did; it's safe to say you were the one who ruined it."

Jay paced the room, pondering Noah's words.

"You got Sullivan," Noah added, "and I understand why you wanted him dead. But this is too far. I told you to stop that night, and you didn't. You gave me no choice."

Jay stopped pacing. "It's funny. I thought that when I found myself in this moment with you, I'd easily kill you on the spot. I now realize that was the wrong decision."

"Why's that?" Noah asked.

"I realize that leaving this town crippled was never the point. It was only part of the fun. Now, after seeing you've failed those people, it's only fair to make them see you as they saw me." Jay pulled a blade from his boot. "Defeated."

Jay's blade ripped through Noah's cheeks like wet paper, entering one side and exiting the other. Noah's scream was dampened by the blood that sprayed from his torn mouth. The blade retracted with Jay's firm pull, and Noah sank into his seat. He groaned, trying not to pump air through the fresh wounds. Breathing through his nose was a small aid for the pain. Spit and blood leaked from his lips.

"To be honest, Noah, I never really expected to last this long. I never wanted to make a grand escape. I just needed to make sure you remember."

The knife swung, piercing Noah's hand.

He screamed again, unable to control the volume this time. Spit and blood gurgled with the shriek. Tears formed in his eyes.

Jay pulled the blade out. "Brother, wouldn't you say the Kirk name is immortal after today?"

Simon nodded.

Branches snapped outside. Jay and Simon glared in the direction of the sound.

"Go check it out," Jay commanded.

Simon pulled out his gun, checking his ammo to confirm he was ready for any impending battle.

He walked to the door and cautiously peeked out. He kept low to avoid surprises that wouldn't play out in his favor. There was a knock against the side of the cabin.

"Hello? Yoohoo."

Simon pushed the door open, swinging his gun toward the noise.

Magnusson leaned against the cabin, waving one hand while the other still applied pressure to his stab wound. His face was white, and blood stained his pants to his knees.

"Stab wound wasn't enough, huh?" Simon asked.

"I wanted to return the favor." Magnusson staggered closer, only stopping when he heard the pistol click.

"You're hardly going to reach me before I put you down." Simon stepped out of the cabin and pressed the pistol to Magnusson's forehead. "This shouldn't hurt at all."

"No, it won't." Magnusson's smile stretched from ear to ear.

A light flickered in the darkness, catching Simon's eye. After staring back, he noticed it was a reflection. A reflection from the rifle scope.

Bang!

Simon's eye socket opened to the size of a baseball. He flew back into the steel mill, painting with the blood flowing from his head.

Jay and Noah looked up in surprise. They had both heard the shot, as it had come from somewhere nearby.

Magnusson rushed into the cabin, pointing his gun at Jay.

"Noah, you okay?" Magnusson asked.

Jay put his pistol to the top of Noah's head. "Quite far from okay if you ask me."

"Drop it, Kirk. This is over. You can't win."

"I did win. We all did. In a single night, four people ripped apart a town to the brink of extinction. In less than twelve hours, I've brought a rebirth to my family name after hearing it dragged through the mud for as long as I can remember."

"You *will* be forgotten," Magnusson promised. "I'll make sure of it."

"Only my body. My legacy is the king of Hyde Cove now," Jay declared.

Adam whistled deep from the woods.

"Noah, duck," Magnusson told his colleague, dropping to the floor.

Noah's reaction was slow, but he heeded Magnusson and bent forward with all his weight, leaning against his binds. He continued until the chair tipped forward, falling down.

Jay stood still, recognizing the empty space between him and the open door. A shot rang out, and for a fraction of a second, his entire world was nothing but pain. Then he flew back into the far wall, slamming his head before crashing to his knees. An open wound in his gut flowed freely, absorbing into the fabric of his shirt. Even when the blood began to pour from him, he didn't seem bothered; he simply smiled.

Magnusson stood over Jay. "Why the smile?"

"Now I'm a memory. An immortal one." Jay slumped forward and emitted one last exhalation, his mortality finally coming to an end.

The sirens echoed through the trees. Magnusson wasn't sure how Adam had gotten back up to assist. Nor did he know help had been dispatched, even though the horror was finally over.

Noah's vision blurred in and out. He saw an army of lights emerge and Adam waving high in the air.

"Over here!" Adam yelled.

The ropes binding Noah to the chair went slack, and he leaned back with relief. Then he looked up to see Magnusson smiling.

"You'll be okay, buddy," he said reassuringly.

Lights invaded the steel mill. Officers swarmed in and surrounded the group. Noah heard their voices through a muffled filter, fading in and out.

"Get EMTs out here right away," said an officer. Magnusson's shirt was soaked in red. His grip on his wounded abdomen loosened, and he toppled forward, falling on his face.

With that, Noah surrendered to unconsciousness. He drifted off, hoping to see Cindy again sooner than later.

CHAPTER 13

WHAT'S LEFT

Three months had passed since that horrible night. Magnusson barely survived the ordeal. He flatlined on the operating table but made a miraculous recovery. He was out on medical leave longer than Noah but eventually returned after a much-needed extended vacation.

Adam Pannella became a new man, having been honored for redeeming his former ways and aiding in Noah's investigation. He didn't care for the added attention besides the occasional free meal at the local diner and being called *Adam the Hero* just about everywhere he went. Most of his previous charges were dropped, and he received steady work aiding in rebuilding the police station. Not to mention doing odd jobs for the damaged properties in town.

It took Noah most of the fall to recover. He took his leave seriously, resting in isolation with little to no assistance. He frequently kept in touch with the few officers who had survived or been transferred from nearby towns to help clean up. Support came in from locals who had returned and volunteers from surrounding communities. They were instructed to investigate Austin's bomb threat thoroughly, but none were ever found. They left it alone, brushing it off as a desperate man's last attempt at spreading fear.

More than half of Hyde Cove's residents had returned to their homes and started to resume their everyday lives. Most local businesses were forced to close due to lack of personnel, and people weren't ready to start again. Some businesses whose owners hadn't survived never recovered from the damages left by the Kirk brothers and were left to fade with time. Still, given all that happened, people didn't give up, found their footing again, and maintained a level of normality.

Donations were received, fundraisers were held, and Hyde Cove made steady progress in returning to normal.

The bodies of the Kirk family were cremated and poured into the river where Jay was thought to have died all those years ago. Though the town fought against the idea, Noah did it to symbolize moving on from the brother's reign of terror, to let their ashes move on from a town that never really gave them what they truly wanted.

Noah sat in the park, admiring the warm fall foliage decorating the trees. Some of the *Grand Reopening* signs on the bakery and several restaurants swayed in the breeze. Magnusson, who spotted his Lieutenant, came to see Noah and sat beside him.

"Lieutenant. Glad to see you taking in the new sights," Magnusson said.

"It's Noah. You know that."

Magnusson nodded. "You're a better man for everything and have been since you were appointed. Sullivan would've never seen this town come so far."

"Sullivan would still be leaving early and sneaking snacks from the vending machine when it was refilled."

Magnusson nearly spat out his coffee. "He never really did have it. Not like you."

Noah didn't have the words to respond. He'd lost Cindy in the process of becoming an officer, and he'd nearly died in the horrors of a single night of violence and madness.

"Magnusson, I nearly lost everything I've worked for in the span of a decade. I don't know if I'm really cut out for Lieutenant."

Magnusson stood, pointing at the town. "Look around you. We rebuilt this in a matter of months. No one would've been able to pull this off without you here. Shit, we barely made any progress while you were recovering. Look all around you. Look at these people. They've lost loved ones. Just about every person here. But they're coming out and living, all because you made it possible again. Hyde Cove survived. We all did."

Noah became absorbed with the town, the people, and the revival. The restaurants had people flooding in like any normal weeknight. The park was full of dog walkers, flirting couples, and people sipping hot drinks.

"This all happened because you let it come back. The town didn't die; the people who tried to kill it did."

Magnusson placed a kind hand on Noah's shoulder. "Live in it again. We're here when you need us."

He let go of his Lieutenant, returning to his squad car. He drove toward the station, back to the work that gave his second chance at life purpose and meaning.

Noah sat a bit longer, then walked back to his car. He sat in the driver's seat for a moment before driving to the outskirts of town. Soon he pulled up to the quiet, peaceful cabin to which he gladly retreated after his daily policing.

He dropped his keys on the table and headed for the basement stairs. He walked to the back of his staircase and slid open the bottom drawer of a large filing cabinet. The four masks sat there, still in plastic evidence bags, still plenty stained with dried blood.

"Just making sure you're all still dead," Noah whispered, "just like your name."

Noah kept his doubts locked away in his basement, only to convey that he was doing well when he needed reassurance. He closed the drawer again, turned out the light, and returned to the top of the stairs.

He was okay with distancing himself from the world, the town, and the reality that the Kirks weren't coming back. He put on a proud face when he had to and reminded himself that that night was now a part of history.

Noah felt better when he reached the top of the stairs. That was, until he collapsed. Leaning against the basement door frame, he sobbed. He cried every day, reliving the dread he hid from everyone else. Like clockwork, the masks reminded him that the brothers won in some way, and he couldn't shake it.

LONG LIVE THE KIRK NAME never left the back of Noah's mind, like a blood stain on a carpet that would never come out. He hoped for a better future, but he was never quite sure. He hoped one day it would be. He hoped as much as he could. Hope was the only thing keeping him going.

ABOUT THE AUTHOR

Joseph has been writing since he was eleven years old. He was inspired by the Nickelodeon show *Doug* because he kept a journal at the same age. Since then, Joseph grew to write numerous short stories and found interest in writing screenplays.

Fast forward to his college graduation. Three short films written, produced, and directed with some film festival recognition. His love for writing stories, creating worlds, and developing characters to both admire and detest flourished as he never stopped creating.

Joseph branched off from screenplays when his ideas broadened what the screen could portray. With a collection of stories in his archive and several novels in the works, there's no telling what will come from his mind and expand onto the pages.

With each piece of writing released, Joseph is constantly expanding his creativity while interacting with fellow writers, documenting his journey, reading, and filling his mind with more inspiration for the next story.

ACKNOWLEDGEMENTS

First, I have to start with the usual. Readers, you've given me so much joy in the first year of my convention circuit, that I am entirely a different writer from the start. Thank you. I hope my words move you as your chances have moved me. Family, friends, and coworkers, who share their love, despite not turning a single page. I appreciate the love and care. You root for me, even when you don't consume the horrors. I value your kind words and well wishes. Maybe I'll get to that "You know what you should write about?" idea. Maybe. A few years from now.

My beloved Nadia. You allow me to reach into the darkest parts of my interests, while keeping me floating, soaring, and thriving for better. My best words will always be for you. Thank you for letting me love you, while still reminding me my greatest success is you. Get the snacks ready, I'll be there in a minute!

James, my editor. I knew from meeting you at Living Dead Weekend that there would be a bond from our conversation. Thank you for taking on this project, thank you for your welcoming nature, and thank you for giving me faith in myself I didn't have before. I look forward to many more writing ventures with you.

Many authors, who give me their time, and encourage me. Wesley Southard, Candace Nola, Briana Morgan, Daniel J. Volpe, Jeremy Megargee, Chase Will, and several others I'll admire from afar. I'm deeply a better writer because I've consumed your words, values, and things you wanted to throw at me. See you all at Author Con!

Lastly, but most important, my loving mother. My first reader, my foundation of support, and the reason I want to cry anytime I watch A.I. Hopefully this has earned me another tattoo without your tears.